The Wonderful World of Corkle

by

Betty L. Myer

Illustrations by

Ellis Goodson

outskirts
press

TABLE OF CONTENTS

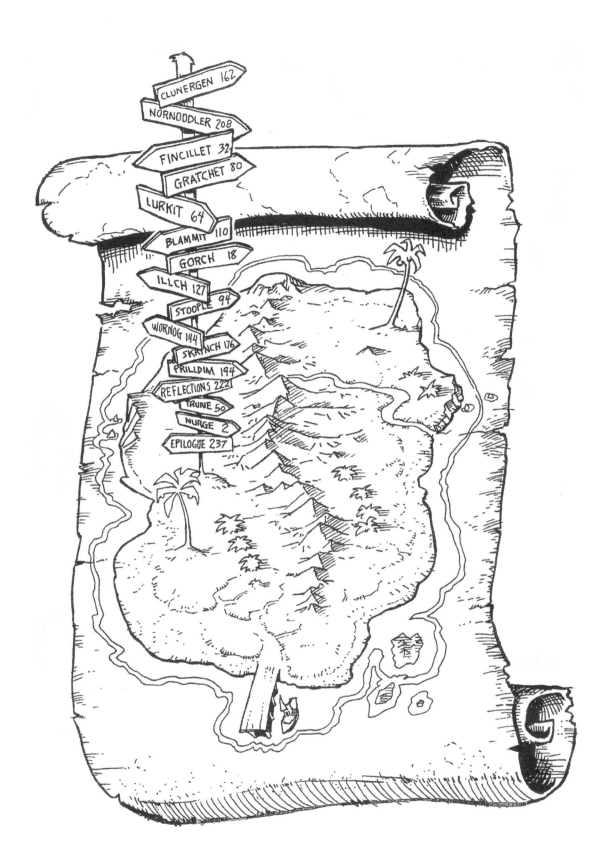

THE WONDERFUL WORLD OF CORKLE

There once was a people who lived on a sphere.
Which developed great trouble that filled them with fear.

From Adam to atom, they called it progress,
Was it forward or backward, that's anyone's guess.

Their language developed from straight "I love you,"
To "We're all confused, now what do we do?"

They had problems aplenty, frustrations galore.
All self-created and they were working on more.

Then "STOP" cried a voice, not loud but emphatic
"Would you accept help to eliminate static?"

Then take just a step, and yet travel far,
To an Island that's no place, but right where you are.

Corkle's an isle on the ocean of thought,
A place you can go and can be what you're not.

If you are a someone you'd rather not be,
The "porple" will help with expediency.

The Porple of Corkle, though not really human,
Have the very same traits that make or undo men.

So stop and relax and imagine this spot,
Where the Porple await to improve on your lot.

PROLOGUE

It was late and the newsroom had grown strangely quiet. The clatter and noise had faded until Taylor Cunningham, the television station's veteran news anchorman, could actually hear the hum of his computer, the pitter patter of the rain outside, and the sounds of traffic on the street below.

Taylor shook himself awake and sighed a heavy, ragged sigh as he glared at the stack of news items that he had to go through before he could call it a wrap and go home.

The pile of papers included stories about the war in Bosnia, the latest threat of Saddam Hussein in the Persian Gulf, the still boiling situation in Haiti, the conflict between Israel and the Palestinians, the murder of a five-year-old in a public housing complex in Chicago. There were more. A drive-by shooting that left a little girl injured, stories about assault, child abuse, robbery, embezzlement, and gang violence. Taylor put his head in his hands and shut his eyes for a moment.

"What's happening to America and our world?" he asked himself. There were still the Washington news stories to go over. Stories of moral corruption, as both political parties promote their own selfish interests, and make promises that everyone knows will never be kept. From his desk drawer, he pulled a facial tissue and rubbed his watery eyes. It had been a long day. He wondered to himself, "Has it always been this bad? What has happened to the positive side of journalism? Where are the inspiring stores like the moon landing and the first shuttle into space?"

Bill Sawyer, Taylor's co-anchorman, called out as he prepared to leave. "Don't work too late Taylor." he said as he pushed his chair into place at his desk. "See you in the morning and don't forget to turn on the alarm system when you leave."

Taylor nodded, then got up slowly and went into the lounge. He mixed himself some instant coffee, took a couple of sips, and then went back to his desk, coffee in hand. There he would face the unpleasant task of preparing the stories for the morning broadcast. Finally, he was down to the last three items. It was going to be a hassle to keep awake long enough to get it finished. Then, a caption caught his eye: "Mysterious island harbors secret to problems."

Taylor buried his face in his hands. "Maybe I'm just tired." He laid his head down on his folded arms with the idea of a short nap and he almost dozed off, but the Island story intrigued him. He shook his head to stay awake. This story demanded his attention. He read on, "Our sources have reported an island called "Corkle, which is not on the map, but certainly exists on the ocean of thought." Taylor's attention was captured in a hurry. "What kind of news reporting is this?" he said out loud.

Continuing the story he read, "There have been reports of exciting changes in those persons who have been contacted by personalities known as "The Porple from Corkle." These inhabitants of Corkle are dedicated to resolving problems for today's mixed up members of the human race.

Taylor threw down the papers, slapped his hand on his desk, and said aloud "This is a joke, this is ridiculous. I cannot believe any of this!"

There was a rustling sound which caused Taylor to look around and listen. Hi eyes finally rested on the top of the computer. There sat an incredible looking bluebird, who was glaring down at him. When their eyes finally made contact, the bird cocked his head to one side and spoke, "And what part of "Porple from Corkle" don't you believe?"

Taylors astonished expression held a long moment before he finally answered. "All of this. It's fantasy. You cannot report this. People today want the truth."

"What do you mean?" said the bird, "you reporters give your listeners fantasy all the time. Don't slam the door in your own face Taylor. This is the truth. Why not come to Corkle with me and find out for yourself?"

"And just how do you propose that I do that?" Amazed and confounded that he was having this conversation in the first place. Taylor leaned back, shut his eyes and relaxed. Then somehow, he let go. Exhaustion had taken its toll and the next thing he knew he was on the dock on the Island of Corkle and was being welcomed by fifteen funny little characters, all at once.

I'm an expert on crime," said one. "Let me tell you about the time…"

He was stopped by another, "I'll help you get rid of worry", he said.

"But wait" the bird that brought Taylor spoke, "I'm the bird that has nerve to spare that helps you do things that would wouldn't dare.

"It's very important to listen." Said another. All of a sudden, they were all pushing towards Taylor, each one eager to tell his own story.

Finally Taylor shouted, "HOLD IT! You guys are all talking at once." Let's go over to that park there and relax." He pointed to a pretty park nearby where benches offered a place to sit. "Now" he started, "I need to hear your stores one at a time… Let's see. How about you?" Taylor pointed at one of the Porple who was wearing roller blades and thick glasses.

"Let's hear your story first. Then, I'll take the time to hear from all of you one at a time."

This little character that Taylor indicated smiled and stepped forward. My name is Nurge." He began.

THE NURGE

In a room full of shelves lives Nurge with his books,
And he's read everything from travel to cooks.

His volumes are worn from the use of their pages,
He's bright with the wisdom passed down through the ages

When ever he's working the time simply flies,
Depend upon Nurge for word to the why's.

He's summarized sums that will add up to say,
He knows all the knowledge clear up to today.

Nurge also has answers in files just to use,
With yesses and no's and maybe's to choose.

If thought collecting is taxing your mind,
Ask Nurge for the help that you'd like to find.

NURGE AND THE TWINS

Don and Dan Eckert had been talking about it for days. "We just won't show" said Don, and Dan nodded his head in agreement. They were discussing not showing up for school.

The Eckert brothers were twins, and according to their parents, what one didn't think of the other one did. Most of the time Donald led the way, while Daniel enthusiastically followed.

The twins and their family lived in East Texas in a beautiful piney woods area. The woods were a real temptation, certainly a lot more fascinating than school, at least that's the way the twins looked at it.

On this particular morning the twins had left home at the regular time. They were almost at the bus stop when Don said, "C'mon, let's do it, you know, let's skip school."

Dan said, "Really?" He looked around a little uncomfortable with the idea.

"Really," said Don. "This is the perfect opportunity. We'll hide, and when the bus stops for us, Mr. Nelson will think we are sick or got to school another way. We'll be back at this spot about the time the bus lets us off in the afternoon. No one will be the wiser. Come on, Dan, it'll be easy, and lots of fun."

"Well, I don't know if we should, but if you say so Don, let's do it." said Dan, grinning at his brother. He turned to listen, "What's that? Is that the bus now?"

They heard the sound of the school bus climbing up the hill and they both made a dive for the thicket nearby to hide in. They could hardly suppress the giggles as they heard the squeak of the brakes when the bus stopped. Mr. Nelson blew the horn several times, then gave up and chugged on up the hill. There were several more stops to make before he deposited the children at school.

Now coming out of their hiding place, and brushing themselves off, Dan turned to Don and said, "well genius now what? Looks like we have all day to do nothing."

"We could go fishing," offered Don.

"No good," said Dan. "We'd be discovered right away if we went home for our poles. Besides, what would we do with the fish we caught?"

"What makes you think we'd catch any. We're not that good at fishing. What we could do is just explore the woods, and go down the creek where we picnic sometimes. We'll probably think of something along the way." Don looked at his brother then nudged him and said, "Let's go, this is going to be fun, and time's a wastin'. "

The twins picked up their lunch pails, and turned toward the trail that led into the woods and to the creek which was their favorite spot to hang out.

Spring was just beginning to show. Little shoots of every conceivable shade of green were everywhere. A few dogwood trees already had blossoms and the birds were busy gathering materials for their nests.

It was quite a walk back into the forest to the creek. The boys laughed, sang, and talked as they walked along. When they heard the bubbly enthusiasm of the creek as it flowed over rocks and debris on its path to the river a few miles away, they were grateful to be at their destination. It was a warm and sunny day with an incredibly blue sky and a few clouds. Don and Dan flopped down on the grassy bank alongside the creek. They laid back and for a while just rested and gazed at nature's abundance all around them. There was a stir of a breeze, and the air was just perfect for a short nap. It had been a long hike and after a short snooze, the boys awakened.

Don looked at his brother and said, "Are you hungry?"

Dan smiled, "I'm always hungry, you know that."

"Then let's eat lunch." said Don. With that they sat up and looked into their lunch pails to see what their mom had put in. As usual they were filled with the nourishing things that their mother had always packed for them, hearty sandwiches, fruit, and home-made cookies, plus a couple of snacks. They ate slowly, savoring every bite, and when they finished, each of them felt stuffed. They lay back on the grass and relaxed.

Suddenly, Dan, who was intent on the changing patterns of the clouds above, asked his brother, "What makes clouds form puffy instead of in streaks?"

"What brought that up?" asked Don. "How would I know? What a question! Why do you ask?"

"Oh, I was just wondering. Sometimes clouds make pictures and I was wondering just how they do it," said Dan.

"There are a lot of mysteries here in the forest," said Don, "like why is the grass always green? If it is alive, that is. What makes it turn yellow and die in the fall, only to become a green carpet again in the Spring?"

"Yeah," said Dan "and why are rocks different colors?"

"And why do the trees lose their leaves in the fall, only to grow new ones in the spring?" said Don.

The twins thought of question after question. They were laid back, half asleep, listening to the lazy buzz of insects at work when it happened. They heard an "ahem." The first thing they thought of was that their little vacation from school had been discovered. Then Dan spotted him.

There he sat on the big rock near them, with his roller blades thrown over his shoulder, adjusting his thick glasses.

"Look," said Don, "we have company."

"What's he want and who is he?" asked Dan.

"What I want is an explanation from you two," said the little man inspecting his fingernails. "Since you were wondering, my name is Nurge. I live in a room full of shelves with my books. I'm out today enjoying the woods and the beautiful weather. As I came through the woods I overheard the two of you asking each other questions and reflecting on the answers. The place to get answers is in school. What are you doing here on a school day anyway?" Nurge looked at one and then the other as he talked. "Well, why aren't you two in school? he demanded, "You certainly aren't sick, and you're definitely not on a field trip."

"We just decided not to go," said Don.

"That's right," added Dan.

"Now that you are here, with nothing in particular to do, are you having a good time?" asked Nurge.

"Well, er— ah, we,..." Don stammered.

"No, we're not having a good time," said Dan. "We're bored, bored, bored."

"Why didn't you bring along a good book to read?" asked Nurge.

"We didn't think of it," replied Don.

"That's right, we didn't think of it," echoed Dan.

"It seems funny to me that if you two get bored easily, you would elect to skip school. I would think it would be the one place you two would want to go," Nurge went on. "I couldn't help but overhear the questions you two were pondering when I walked up. Don't you know that the answers to all those things can be found in books in the school library?"

"I don't like the library," said Don.

"Me neither" said Dan.

"Why not?" asked Nurge.

"They won't let you talk," said the twins together.

"You're in the library to read, study, and learn. It's hard to do all that if you're talking, besides, you disturb everyone else, and that's not fair. The best thing about the library is that every book can be your own personal adventure," said Nurge.

"What do you mean by that?" asked Don.

"Yeah, what do you mean by that?" repeated Dan.

"You, Dan," Nurge said, pointing at Dan. "You were asking why clouds take different shapes. If you were to open a book on the study of our weather systems it would explain all that."

"Really?" asked Don, now starting to get interested in what Nurge had to say.

"That's right." Nurge went on, "With a little imagining along with what you would read about weather you could take a balloon flight and see the world. You could follow the winds that shape the clouds."

"Wow!" said the twins together.

"Imagine it all," said Nurge, "to watch the sun rise and set and float over the earth with only the sound of the winds. You could watch the weather form. It's all in the books you would find about clouds, wind, weather, that sort of thing. You can pretend any adventure you would like to have just by reading a book."

The twins were fascinated with the idea of adventures. East Texas is great, but there's a whole unexplored world out there. Nurge continued to talk. He had the twin's attention as he told of the many exciting adventures and experiences to be had. All they have to do is to get familiar with the books in their own library. Then, just as suddenly as Nurge had appeared, he stood up and walked around the big rock and disappeared.

The twins stood very still for a few minutes. Then they tiptoed in the direction of the big rock. Don went first, with Dan close on his heels. They looked and looked, but Nurge was gone for sure.

Don turned slowly and looked at his brother, "Do you believe what we just saw?"

Dan shook his head with slow deliberation. "I don't know what to believe, but I sure love Nurge's stories about adventure. I'd like to try it. You know, try to have an adventure with a book."

"Me too," said Don. "You know it really wouldn't hurt to check out the school library tomorrow. Maybe we've been missing something."

"No, it really wouldn't hurt," echoed Dan. The twins had been given a whole new outlook regarding the library and school.

Dan and Don finally decided that it was time to head back through the forest to the bus stop. The time passed quickly as they discussed what book adventures they would have first. Don talked of an adventure on the high seas in a beautiful sailing ship. Then he suddenly realized that he would have to learn how to navigate, how to cope with the sails to make the best use of the winds.

"No matter," he said to his brother, "there's gotta be a book on that too!"

They laughed as they stepped out of the woods on to the road that led home. Then they almost ran into the arms of their father standing right in front of them with his hands on his hips, glaring at both of them.

"Uh oh," the twins said together.

"You better believe 'uh oh'," roared their father. "Where in the world have you two been? You're going to give your mother and me gray hair before our time. Mrs. Dwire called from school to see if you were all right. She was worried when you didn't arrive at school. Needless to say, your mother and I were out of our minds. We have been everywhere looking for you." The more Mr. Eckert talked, the redder he got. "We are going to let Mrs. Dwire figure out a suitable punishment for the two of you. Now, where have you been and what in the dickens have you been doing?"

Don and Dan looked up at their father. Their shaking knees betrayed how they felt. Finally Don summoned the courage to say, "We ah, we went on a nature walk."

Dan looked at him surprised, and then repeated what his brother had offered as an excuse, "Yeah, we went on a nature walk."

"And what wondrous and naturally beautiful things did you see?"

Mr. Eckert asked sarcastically.

"The dogwoods are starting to bloom," said Don, "and we studied the clouds for a while,"

And we saw lots of different colored rocks too," offered Dan "We noticed that the water is deeper in the creek, and..."

Mr. Eckert stopped their recitation, "Enough! enough!" he said. Come on home now, it's time for chores. Your mother has been mighty worried about you. I can promise that if you ever pull a stunt like this again, you won't sit a saddle easy for a week. NOW IS THAT CLEAR?" His voice had risen to thunder again. The twins nodded in unison and followed their father's footsteps in silence.

The next morning as they walked to the bus stop Don said to his brother, "I wonder what kind of punishment we're going to get for skipping school yesterday."

Dan answered, "Maybe we won't get to go out for recess."

"You can think of the worst stuff, but what if we get double home work?" asked Don.

"Oh no, or what if Mrs. Dwire makes us write essays, or sit in the front of the room, or maybe sit next to Mildred?" said Dan.

"What is for sure," said Don, "is that we're in for it. We'll just have to brace ourselves for the worst."

"Yeah", said Dan, "we'll just have to brace ourselves."

But it didn't turn out that way at all. The next morning the principal, Mrs. Dwire, called to them as they walked from the bus toward the school building. "I need to speak to the two of you at once in class-room eight."

Dan and Don looked at each other and Don said quietly, "Well, here it comes.

"Yeah, here it comes," added Dan. They followed Mrs. Dwire down the hall to her room. It was as though they were prisoners being led to the execution. When they reached Mrs. Dwire's room they entered sheepishly as she walked in front of them into the room.

"Sit down, please," she said, as she seated herself behind her desk. She went on, "Daniel and Donald, we must make it very clear to the both of you that skipping school is simply not acceptable and will not be tolerated. Do you understand?"

"Yes ma'am." said both twins together.

Mrs. Dwire fingered the papers in front of her. Boys, these are your progress reports I have in front of me. They are not very impressive. Both of you have a great deal of room to improve on your reading skills. For that reason I'm going to keep you after school for two hours every day in the school library. You will be expected to read at least three books a week, then turn in a written book report on all of them at the end of the week."

Don looked at Dan with a look of surprise, and Dan started to grin widely, but was stopped with a nudge from Don. Mrs. Dwire was eyeing the two of them.

"This is not at all humorous, Daniel. It is very serious, and there will be further punishment if your written assignments are not handed in on time. You will also choose one book to report on orally to the class. Now is all this perfectly clear?" Mrs. Dwire was very stern and her voice had risen considerably.

"Yes ma'am," said the twins.

Mrs. Dwire had not mentioned just how long the so-called punishment would continue, but Dan and Don were ecstatic. As they left the room they turned and smiled and said, "Thank you, Mrs. Dwire."

"You're welcome," said Mrs. Dwire. She felt a shudder, and there was a puzzled look on her face as she thought to herself, "Those two took it pretty well. I wonder what they are up to now."

The rest of the school day was pretty routine. Both boys dug into their school work. They wanted all of their studies completed so that they could use the library time to explore.

Mr. Eckert had made arrangements to pick up the boys after school. The bus would be long gone before the twins were ready to go home.

Don and Dan had it all worked out. They knew the "no talking" rule in the library. In order for them to communicate, they cut numerous pieces of paper, for notes. They were small so as not to attract attention. Yes, this was going to be a lot of fun.

When the two of them walked into the library after school, Miss Lassen, the librarian, looked up with a "What did I do to deserve this" expression. She pointed to the table closest to her and whispered, "Sit here where I can see you."

"Yes ma'am," said the twins together.

The twins were very surprised when Miss Lassen came to their table and sat down. "I have here a list of instructions on how to find the books that you will want to read and take home. The information is all here. Let's really try to make this a positive experience for all of us. I will do all I can to make it pleasant for the two of you. Just ask me if the information you need is not on the paper and I will be pleased to help you anytime." Miss Lassen took her glasses off then and smiled at the two boys. "Remember," she said, cleaning her glasses, "I'm here to help." She got up then and went back behind the check-in counter.

Dan wrote a short note to Don, "Miss Lassen is pretty without her glasses."

Don returned a note to Dan, "She smells good too! Let's be nice."

That first afternoon the boys quietly studied the paper that Miss Lassen had given them. Then they both explored some of the ways to get around the library to obtain information. They hardly looked at each other; they just buried themselves in finding books that looked interesting. Selecting and rejecting, they ventured through the rows of shelves filled with books on every possible subject you could imagine.

Both boys were surprised when Miss Lassen announced that it was time to meet their father out in front of the school. Mr. Eckert was dumbfounded as the two talked of nothing but the things they had discovered in the books they had selected. He couldn't get over the change, but he welcomed it for sure! Still, he had never seen them so fired up about books.

The days flew by, and the boys were having the time of their lives. They were overwhelmed by the discoveries they had already made. There was no time for mischief, to the delight of Mrs. Dwire. They were changing and everyone was very happy about that.

It happened to Dan first. He was standing between two rows of books trying to decide which book on weather he would like to read. Dan thought he saw something move out of the corner of his eye. He looked to see Nurge moving swiftly down through the rows of books on his rollerblades. "I'm not seeing this," Dan muttered to himself, but quicker than he could imagine Nurge came around the corner again and stopped right beside him.

"What are you looking for?" said Nurge peering up at Dan through his thick glasses.

Dan was surprised at himself as he answered. "I'm looking for a good book on weather."

"All three of these books are good," said Nurge, "but this one will be the best one for you since you're only in the fifth grade." Nurge handed Dan the book, and before he could even say thank you, Nurge was down the row and around the corner.

Dan thumbed through the book, and found that Nurge was right, it was great, and easy to read. He took it back to the table where Miss Lassen had seated them. Just after he sat down he felt a bump on the table and looked up to see a wild-eyed Don looking down at him. Don hastily sat down to write and pass a note to his brother.

"You'll never guess who I met back in the rows of books," he wrote.

Dan wrote back, "I know, I saw Nurge too." They smiled at each other in approval.

As the days passed the twins became more and more excited about the things they were learning from books. The quiet was usually broken by "Hey, listen to this!"

The regular classes for Dan and Don became much easier. As they read, their knowledge about all things greatly increased. Mrs. Dwire was delighted with the change in the twins. They were keeping up with their daily assignments, and they gave their oral book reports to an attentive and interested class. Mrs. Dwire wrote glowing remarks on their finished work.

No doubt about it, Nurge had helped the twins change themselves, and they had become outstanding students.

Several months passed, and one Saturday afternoon the twins were at their favorite spot down by the creek in the woods. They were both deep into the books they had brought along to read. Suddenly they heard a rustle behind them. They both looked up to see Nurge come out from around the big rock. He had his roller blades over one shoulder and a knapsack over the other. "I came by the say so-long to you guys," he said.

"Why, where are going?" said Don.

"Where are you going and what for?" said Dan.

"There's a library over near Tyler that needs my help," said Nurge. "You two have all the kids reading here, there's not much for me to do. So you see, it's time for me to move on."

"We'll miss you, Nurge." said Don.

"Yes, we will," echoed Dan. "Come and see us once in a while."

Nurge blinked with pleasure at both of them and said, "You two have made me very proud of you." Then he turned and before the boys could even get to their feet, he was gone.

That's the story of the Twins and Nurge. Maybe the next time you visit your library you might see a quick little man with thick glasses speeding around on roller blades, scooting quietly through the rows of books. If you need help, just ask him. He'll be happy to be your friend.

GORCH

If you have the problem of putting on fat,
And you can't sit yourself in the place you once sat

Let Gorch eat the food that you really don't need,
He feels that he's doing a very good deed.

He'll slick up the beaters and clean up the bowls,
Take care of the crumbs and the leftover rolls.

Both of you know that "Too Fat" is a shame,
He'll help with the sweets that are mostly to blame.

He knows that "think thin" is not just a phrase,
He assists you in knowing your try's not a phase.

Gorch is your diet if you're overweight,
Let him overeat, and you'll start feeling great.

ELIZABETH AND GORCH

Elizabeth's all day shopping trip ended in disaster. She had checked out every shop she knew but found nothing she thought was appropriate to wear on Sunday. Her big weight gain was a shock. Discouraged and disappointed Elizabeth gave into exhaustion and headed home.

"What a bummer," she mumbled to herself as she rode home on the bus, "I can't go on like this... but diets are for the birds... even if they do work they're murder. Besides, after you stop dieting you gain the weight right back, usually plus more."

Elizabeth had a lot going for her, a pretty face, a nicely proportioned figure, a sweet personality and a sharp mind. A people person, she loved social activities, which didn't help the situation because such activities usually involved food which always presented her with a problem. To please her hostess or bolster her confidence or for whatever reason she could think of at the moment, Elizabeth invariably grazed from one platter of food to the next. But afterwards she always felt terrible. Poor Elizabeth, as her scale went up, her self assurance went down.

As Elizabeth slowly climbed the stairs to her apartment, she suddenly remembered that the showing of the new computer line was next Sunday and that she still had nothing to wear. Her heart sank. She put her key in the lock and pushed open the door. Her long time friend and roommate, Marcie Goodwin was stretched out on the couch munching on an apple.

Marcie saw her, jumped up and switched off the television. "Well, how did the shopping go, Liz?"

Elizabeth shook her head, "I saw lots of pretty things, but they just wouldn't do. Gosh, Marcie, I'm so discouraged, I'm really out of shape, I could hardly get up those stairs."

Marcie looked concerned, "I've been telling you, Liz, you need to come to the gym with me and get into a regular physical fitness program. By the way, there's some wonderful apples in the kitchen, want one?"

"I probably shouldn't eat anything at all," responded Elizabeth.

"Don't be silly," said Marcie, "we both know there are hardly any calories in an apple.

After a few minutes Elizabeth headed for the kitchen. "You know, Marcie, I could eat something. I didn't stop for lunch, and I'm starved. Is there any more of the lasagna?"

"I guess so," Marcie said following her into the kitchen. "I don't touch lasagna, it makes me feel stuffed. There's still some of the salad, or do you want some fruit yogurt? I bought some of the small low cal snack meals today. They're not bad, wanna try one?"

Elizabeth suddenly felt her appetite raging out of control. "No thanks" she said rummaging around in the refrigerator, stacking a generous portion of the lasagna onto a plate, putting it into the microwave, adding rolls slathered with butter and wolfing it all down with both hands as though it had been a month since her last meal. When the plates were empty, in spite of a momentary twinge of guilt, again the door to the refrigerator swung open. "Lets see now," said Elizabeth rubbing her hands together, "for dessert, aha, cheesecake, and a piece of apple pie, and some pumpkin pie," Unable to decide which one she preferred, she ate them all.

Topping her sumptuous meal off with a diet drink, Elizabeth joined Marcie in front of the T.V. With a tray full of snacks. Marcie watched in horror as Elizabeth quickly demolished every morsel.

When she was finished Elizabeth patted her tummy and sighed, "Oh Marcie that was so good... and so bad, I haven't solved anything... and I feel so fat. I don't deserve any new clothes. The trouble is, I don't think about going on a diet until I've eaten everything in sight. Sometimes I really hate myself." Tears filled her eyes as she gazed at Marcie, so thin, so in control, so in charge of everything in her life.

"Liz, you're your own worst enemy, "Marcie snapped," and crying is not going to help."

Elizabeth stood in front of the full length mirror on the closet door, "What am I going to do Marcie? I don't know where to start! I'm at least a size eighteen and growing."

"If you want me to help, I will." said Marcie, "but I won't fight with you, It's up to you. You have to do it yourself." She abruptly turned and disappeared into the bathroom.

Elizabeth flopped down on the couch to watch T.V., wondering why all the commercials were about food... and the ones that weren't seemed to be about diets. "I just can't seem to get away from it," she thought to herself, "It's on my mind all the time. Couch potato, that's me all right. I'm even beginning to look like a potato. Food and T.V., what a defeating combination. I suppose I should turn the T.V. off and read, at least I would have control of what I'm putting into my mind."

Marcie came out of the bathroom dressed in her pajamas. She went over to the couch and hugged Elizabeth. "I'm sorry, Liz, I didn't mean to be so hard on you, I love you, but sometimes I don't know what to do. Please let me help. It's so hard to see you this way." She started toward the bedroom, and paused to look back at Elizabeth, "Please let me help you get your life under control"

Elizabeth smiled at her and said, "I will Marcie, thanks for your understanding."

Marcie gave her another hug, went into the bedroom and shut the door.

Elizabeth settled herself on the couch, and thought about her friendship with Marcie, thinking she was lucky to have her support. She used the remote to click, click, and click again. There wasn't much to watch, certainly nothing that she wanted to see. She yawned, and suddenly felt sleepy. "I ate too much," she thought imagining herself a four hundred pound side show fat lady as she dozed off.

A loud blast from a T.V. commercial about ice cream and ice cream cakes rudely awakened Elizabeth. She was startled to see a fat little figure oozing himself out of a banana split. "What in the world?" she gasped, "now I'm seeing things."

A flabbergasted Elizabeth watched in fascination as the fat little figure moved out of the television screen over to the remains of her snack tray. "How'd you do that?" she demanded.

"Is easy" the little man said. "It happens when I'm needed"

Elizabeth was mesmerized… "Who are you? What are you doing in our television set, and how did you get out? Where did you come from?"

"Not so fast," said the little man. "First of all my name is Gorch, and I come from the Island of Corkle. I'm here to help you with your eating troubles."

"Wait a minute," said Elizabeth, "I have no trouble eating, that's my problem."

"That's where I come in." said Gorch, "I will eat the food that you don't need. As you can see, there's plenty of room," he thumped his belly.

"When you start to overeat, or eat something that's not good for you, I'll do the eating for you. You must learn to think thin Elizabeth… When you look in the mirror, don't look for a fat reflection, but see yourself as a beautiful size eight."

Elizabeth Sighed, "I only wish I could."

"One of your problems is that you were always rewarded with food when you were a child, right?"

"Yes, that's right, but what does that have to do with anything."

Gorch cut her off, "Elizabeth, when something is bothering you, and you need a pat on the back, you turn to food for comfort. That's where

I come in. I'll eat the goodies for you and this will give you confidence. There are no calories in feeling good about yourself. Between us we eliminate the middle man. Get it, Elizabeth? Middle man?" Gorch held his middle and laughed, and Elizabeth joined him with a giggle.

"How is this possible?" said Elizabeth, getting serious again.

"You will learn that you don't have to look to food for comfort, you need food only to nourish your body. This whole concept must begin in your mind." Gorch grinned at her.

"What do you mean?" asked Elizabeth.

"Let me ask you. Did you feel prettier and more accepted when you were forty pounds lighter?"

"Of course, my clothes fit better, and were easier to find. Boys whistled instead of making their "wide load" remarks. I'm really in a 'catch 22' position. I overeat to feel better, but end up feeling worse because I pig out and betray myself." Elizabeth was crushed, and the "full" feeling from the lasagna wasn't helping.

Gorch looked at her. "I know that you feel terrible right now, but we're going to change this habit together."

"How are we going to do that?" asked Elizabeth.

"We're going to do it with teamwork and substitutions!" Smiled Gorch.

"Substitutions? What substitutions?"

Gorch started to pace. "Let's see," he said, "let's list some, like walking. Yes, walking is good, as well as swimming and bicycling. You could start working out at the gym with Marcie, that would be helpful. And take a dance class, that burns calories. All these things are good, Elizabeth, because they are exercise, and exercises lessen your craving for food. Treat yourself to a day at the beauty parlor, not the ice cream parlor."

Elizabeth laughed at that suggestion.

"Go to the library and look up something exciting, like a cruise or a trip to Tahiti. Get a manicure, the ladies tell me that's a real treat.

Spend a half hour in a bubble bath with your favorite fragrance and a good magazine, maybe one of the light cooking magazines. Make yourself familiar with tasty light foods that don't expand your waistline." Gorch listed the things on his fingers. "Drink lots of water, I mean lots of water, eight glasses a day, at least. You can't fill your belly with food if it's full of water, besides your body needs water to wash out your insides. More than anything love yourself Elizabeth. When you look in the mirror see yourself as a size eight, not what you see now. Get the idea? In Corkle we call it Imagineering."

Elizabeth groaned "How can I possibly be strong enough to do all that?"

"You're gonna do it with my help," said Gorch." One thing you need to know is who your friends are."

"I don't understand, what you mean?" asked Elizabeth.

Those who would 'force feed' you into eating things that aren't good for you are really not your friends. Neither are those who try to encourage you to 'just taste.' Be assertive. Associate with people who are in control of their lives and most of all learn to just say no."

"I'll try if you'll help me." said Elizabeth.

Gorch put a hand on Elizabeth's shoulder, "The most important thing is to love yourself each day just as you are. When you look in that full length mirror, see Elizabeth Thomas, beauty queen. Do you understand what I mean?"

"Well yes, sort of," said Elizabeth.

"Make a list of what you should and shouldn't eat." smiled Gorch. "Comb through the nutrition books and select things you like. The more you expose yourself to healthier foods, the more you'll like them. Eat only when you're hungry, and when you do eat, eat only until satisfied, not stuffed."

Elizabeth frowned, "What do I do when I come face to face with a coconut cream pie?"

"Call me, and I'll eat it for you." said Gorch with a wink. "Be sure and let me know, even if it's an emergency. Don't worry about me overeating because my magic belly stays one size."

With that Gorch took a small rug out of his pocket, shook it out to make a bridge into the television set, and disappeared into a cheeseburger.

All of a sudden the T.V. screen shifted to a test pattern. Elizabeth sat up with a start and looked at her watch, it was l: 30 AM. Her head was reeling. "Did I really see that fat little fellow?" she asked herself, "I must have been dreaming. But he was so real, so life like, I just know he was here."

Elizabeth turned off the television and got ready for bed. She was just starting to fall asleep when she suddenly jumped out of bed turned on the lights back on, went to the writing desk to leave a note for Marcie which read, "Wake me in the morning and we'll run together."

The next morning Marcie shook her awake. "Come on, sleeping beauty, let's run."

Elizabeth protested sleepily," Good God Marcie go away, it's the middle of the night."

Marcie had no mercy, "Up and at 'em," she said, as she pulled up the blinds, threw back the covers, and opened the window. "You wanted to get your life in order, this is the first step"

Elizabeth groaned as she put on her sweats, bent over to lace her shoes, and staggered out the door after Marcie.

"Since this is your first day we won't run too far, or too fast, a mile should be plenty." said Marcie.

"A mile?" asked Liz, "I don't know if I can even walk a mile."

"Rule one, no griping. Rule two, keep up and shut up. Rule three, keep on keeping on until it feels good" puffed Marcie.

Elizabeth shouted between gasps of air, "Marcie I can't go any further"

"Yes you can, don't stop now we're almost there."

By the time they got back to the apartment, Elizabeth was exhausted.

After a few minutes rest she felt a lot better. "Gee Marcie I feel good," said Elizabeth...

Marcie responded, "Of course you do, exercise is exhilarating. Now, do some stretching, and take your shower. I'm having some oatmeal, will you join me?"

"Sure" answered Liz, surprised at her own answer, since she usually had Danish for breakfast.

"How about meeting me at George's Salad Bar for lunch today,"

"Sure, I'd love it", said Elizabeth knowing she would need more suport by lunch time.

When Elizabeth got to work she noticed a young man at her desk. "I wonder who that is," she said to herself," those shoulders don't look familiar to me". Then he turned around to look at her and she almost lost her composure. He was the most attractive man she had ever seen.

"Hello," he said," are you Elizabeth Thomas?"

She spoke with more confidence than she was feeling, "Yes, may I help you?" Then she thought to herself, "Gee I wish I were skinny."

"I'm Luke Beauman from the home office. They've sent me here to help with the show. You have done a great job on the set-up plan. Do you suppose we could talk about it over lunch?"

Elizabeth hesitated. She didn't want to turn him down, because she knew he might be important to the advancement of her career. On the other hand she had made a date with Marcie, and wouldn't be able to reach her by phone before noon. Besides having lunch with someone as good looking as him would put her into a feeding frenzy. "I'm so sorry Mr. Beauman I already have plans for lunch."

Mr. Beauman looked disappointed. "That's O.K., maybe we can make it another time."

Preparations for the computer show kept Elizabeth very busy all morning long. When lunch time came around she hurried out of the building and dashed down 6th street to meet Marcie, she couldn't wait to tell Marcie about her handsome new co-worker. The salad, to her surprise, tasted fabulous.

Elizabeth spent the whole afternoon working with Luke Beauman. He was a nice person and didn't seem to notice that she was overweight. They made a great team, each one complementing the other in ideas, energy, and talents.

The next day flew by quickly as Elizabeth dove into her work. Luke Beauman had many constructive suggestions and was a tremendous help. By quitting time Elizabeth felt she had things pretty well pulled together, but what to wear was still a problem.

Luke interrupted her thoughts, "Well, Elizabeth, do you think you know me well enough now to have dinner with me this evening?"

Elizabeth cringed, she thought of Gorch, then decided to be honest, "You know, Luke, I would love to, but I really don't think I'd be much fun. I'm trying to deal with a weight problem."

"Great!" said Luke much to her surprise. "I certainly know how that goes. Believe me, I've been there. I lost over 60 pounds last year, and I still have to watch it"

"You?" exclaimed Elizabeth, "You overweight?"

"Me," said Luke. "My doctor scared me to death when he found out how much weight I had gained. He explained what I was doing to my health, and put me on a strict diet. To tell the truth I wasn't happy about my appearance and lack of energy. So you see, I know what you're going through, I've been through it myself. Trust me to find a restaurant that will suit us both."

Elizabeth beamed as she gave him instructions how to get to her house.

The evening was great. Luke took Elizabeth to a lovely dinner house that catered to healthy choices. They discovered that they had a world of things in common, Elizabeth even asked Luke about what she should wear on Sunday. He suggested that she choose a dress to flatter her coloring, something flowing that she could belt in later, and then a touch of outrageous jewelry.

When dinner was over the waiter brought a tray of scrumptious goodies for their consideration. Elizabeth looked at the tray with a watering mouth—then all of a sudden she saw a figure ooze out of the cream puff. Gorch! She shook her head then and said "No thank you." thinking to herself, "He remembered. Oh thank you, Gorch!"

At the end of the evening Elizabeth said to Luke, "How can I thank you for being so understanding?"

Luke smiled and said, "Elizabeth, you will soon feel much better about yourself. Self control helps you feel beautiful inside—which leads to external beauty, but you don't need any help there."

After they said good night Elizabeth sat down to tell Marcie all about her evening. Then later alone, she thought," It's wonderful, first Gorch, then Luke,...how lucky can I get?"

Without thinking, Elizabeth flipped on T.V., and to her astonishment there sitting in the middle of a chocolate cake was Gorch.

"How was your date?" he asked, licking his fingers.

"Wonderful, Luke is the most understanding person," said Elizabeth.

"Is that right?" said Gorch, "And who do you think helped him dump the 60 pounds? He would have told you, but he still feels a little strange about his acceptance of me as a friend. He's afraid someone might think he's crazy."

Elizabeth giggled, "I can understand that. That's why I didn't mention you, either."

"Remember Elizabeth," said Gorch, "just take it ounce by ounce." Then Gorch was gone and Elizabeth faced the T.V. test pattern again.

She sat there with a wistful smile on her face and thought, "What a wonderful life!" She looked down at herself, "I feel skinny already."

FINCILLET

Delusions of grandeur are really a bore,
That mask that you wear is a very dull chore.

The things you admire on the ladder of merit,
Are apt to subdue all the best you inherit.

You're up in the air without a support,
You're stepping on toes and call it a sport.

You have to be "first", ONE isn't so great,
Nine numbers in all God saw to create.

Fincillet will help you get back down to earth,
Where you can be safe in your very own berth.

Such a waste of your time when you're not being you,
Fincillet is false so you can be true.

LISA AND FINCILLET

Lisa stood before the full-length mirror and gazed with admiration at her reflection. Her incredible auburn hair, which had been styled to look casually curly caused her large green eyes to sparkle with self-approval. Her makeup was flawless, and her hands were tipped with perfect fingernails artistically done to look natural. Lisa's smile displayed her dimples as she let her eyes travel down to take in the soft curves, all in the right places. She sighed, "Very feminine, the winner for sure, I am the perfect Miss Evergreen County" she whispered.

The past week had been hectic, so many details to attend to. Lisa had exhausted every detail and everyone around her to assure her winning the pageant. She had been to the voice coach each day to go over her speech, 'Making the Best of Your Perfection.' The coach had challenged the topic, but Lisa brushed him away with, "You are what you are, why hide it?" She was sure that anyone who saw what she saw in the mirror would agree.

As she buffed her nails, Lisa smiled to herself and thought about the events of the past week.

Lisa was uptight, and her temper tantrum had been heard all over the salon. The first hairdresser had not understood her instructions, and Lisa, in a most unlady like way, called her stupid, without training, and said her technique was unacceptable. She demanded another operator, and insisted the whole ordeal be done all over again. The first operator left for the day, she was so unstrung and devastated, she couldn't complete her schedule.

Lisa had gone to have her gown fitted. The seamstress was very capable, but by the time she had spent an hour with Lisa, she was completely unglued. Lisa just didn't seem to be able to work with people without insulting them. Her rude and aggressive attitude had everyone on edge. By the time the fitting was over the seamstress was in tears, and Lisa had slammed the door on her way out of the building.

The knock on the door interrupted Lisa's thoughts. "Who is it?" she asked.

"It's Mom, Lisa, lunch is ready," said her mother.

"OK, I'm coming," said Lisa, following her mother into the kitchen, which was filled with the wonderful smell of homemade soup.

Mrs. Lindsay had made a plate of turkey sandwiches, little cups of hearty soup, and there were brownies for dessert.

"Mother I hope you don't expect me to eat all that, you know I'm trying to watch my weight," exclaimed Lisa.

"Why not, Queen Lisa?" chimed her little sister, Nancy. "Does her royal highness prefer something from the palace's private stock?"

Lisa glared at Nancy, "Mother, can't you put this little earthworm back in its can?"

"Now girls, don't fuss at each other," said Mrs. Lindsay. "You can eat as much as you want and set the rest aside." She looked at her younger daughter, "Nancy, don't tease your sister."

While they ate their lunch in silence, Lisa's mind went back over the events of the past week. Luckily, in the beauty shop she had over heard Mary Turner, another pageant contestant, describing a gown she had seen at Harwood's Department Store. Lisa had listened with fascination, it was exactly what she had been looking for.

Mary had said, "I would have bought it on the spot, but I didn't have enough money, so I asked the sales girl to hold it for me until this afternoon. As soon as I'm finished here, I'll run down and try it on before anyone else has a chance to see it."

Lisa pushed everyone to hurry so that she could get out of the salon and wasted no time rushing down to Harwood's. The clerks were dumbfounded when Lisa demanded to see the dress that Mary had described.

"I don't know how you knew we had it," said the first sales lady as she hurried into the back room. "We just got it in last evening." She brought out the dress, and Lisa caught her breath. Fashioned with a full circular pink chiffon skirt which was cut on the bias, the skirt looked endless as it swirled around. It was gathered onto a matching pink satin bodice which was encrusted with pink Austrian crystals and tiny seed pearls. The neckline was off the shoulder, revealing the lovely neck and shoulders that were Lisa's. Lisa turned and turned, to see every angle, the dress was perfection.

"Are you sure this is the only one of it's kind?" asked Lisa. The sales lady assured her that it was.

Lisa had just taken off the dress when a second salesperson appeared in the dressing room, "I'm afraid we have a problem," she said. "Mary Turner asked me to hold this dress for her. She tried it on just a few hours ago."

Lisa stopped her, "Did she give you a deposit?"

The salesperson stammered, "Uh, well ah, no." she reddened, "but..."

"No but's about it," said Lisa. "I have to have it, it's mine. I have the cash right here in my bag."

The two sales ladies were appalled that Lisa would buy the dress knowing that Mary had asked them to hold it. But Lisa was there, cash in hand, so there was little anyone could do about it. As Lisa left the store she smiled to herself triumphantly.

"Hey Queenie," Nancy's voice interrupted Lisa's daydreaming. "Pass the sandwiches please."

"Good heavens, mother, look at her, she eats like a pig." said Lisa.

"Hey, this is my first sandwich," Nancy defended herself. "Besides, I'm hungry. I've been helping Mom this morning while you've been in conference with your mirror."

"I have to be careful of my fingernails," said Lisa. "I can't break one now, I don't know if I can get another appointment.."

"Oh, la-de-da," said Nancy.

Lisa looked at her little sister with disgust, "You know Nancy, you really need to start taking care of yourself. Your looks are going to need all the help they can get." "Who cares," said Nancy. "My friends like me just the way I am." She grabbed a sandwich from the tray and headed out the back door. "I'm going out back to the picnic table Mom, all this fuss about glamour and beauty gives me nausea."

"Poor little twirp," said Lisa, "She's so plain, I hope she can grow out of it some day."

"Your little sister is sweet and loving, Lisa. You'd do well to adopt some of her habits and attitudes. She has a lot of friends who really care about her, and it doesn't surprise me. Nancy is always doing something for someone else, and she's kind and considerate to everyone." said Mrs. Lindsay.

Lisa went back to her own thoughts. "Who needs friends?" she wondered. "When I win the fifteen thousand dollars from the pageant I'll be able to do some of the things I have always wanted to do. I'll be able to travel, maybe go to New York, Hollywood, or Paris. Still, fifteen thousand dollars won't go very far, but it will give me a chance to have a fling before I go off to college."

The phone rang and Lisa carefully picked it up. In her most practiced voice she said "Hello, Lindsay residence, Lisa speaking."

"Hello Lisa, this is Mary Turner. I couldn't believe it when Harwoods called to tell me that you had bought my dress. You knew they were holding it for me.

"Your dress?" said Lisa, "I'm sorry, but that was and is MY dress. I was there first with the cash, so it's mine."

"You heard us talking about it at the beauty shop, or you wouldn't even have known the dress was there." said Mary, on the verge of tears.

"So?" answered Lisa.

"So," said Mary, "I just wanted to let you know that I know you bought the dress right out from under me. You overheard me talking to Sue, and you rushed right down to Harwood's to buy it before I could get back with the money. It was a pretty rotten thing to do Lisa."

"Not at all," said Lisa. "That dress is made for me. You couldn't possibly do it justice. What I did was make the most out of an opportunity. I had been looking for the right dress everywhere, and there it was. Blame yourself, Mary, maybe you need to learn to keep your mouth shut."

The phone clicked on the other end as Mary hung up. "Mary isn't too smart," smiled Lisa to herself, "never let them see you sweat."

Lisa called to her mother, "I'm taking the car, mother, I have to pick up the shoes I had dyed, and stop by to get the regulation swim wear at Morgan's."

"All right," said Mrs. Lindsay, "but I'll need the car in about an hour."

"No problem," answered Lisa. She was wearing a pair of white gabardine slacks, and a pale yellow silk blouse. Grabbing a matching pale yellow cashmere sweater, she headed out the door.

Lisa slid behind the wheel of the car and she thought to herself, "The absolute nerve of Mary to call me. That was tacky. I wouldn't have lowered myself."

As Lisa drove through the familiar streets toward the shoe store she glanced down at the fuel gauge and noticed that the tank was almost empty. "Better fill up," she said to herself, and turned left into the service station.

"Oh heck," thought Lisa, "There's Ben Peterson. Ever since he took me to the prom he thinks I'm his girl or something. I hope he doesn't see me." She bounced out of the car, and came around to the gas pump. Carefully she lifted the nozzle from its cradle, and gingerly unscrewed the gas cap.

Suddenly she was startled when a big hand took the nozzle from her and a voice said, "Here, let me do that, you might get dirty."

Lisa looked up over her shoulder, "great!" she thought. It was Ben. She pulled away as his hand touched hers. "Ahgh, don't touch me with those dirty hands, Ben. My goodness, look at you, you're filthy."

Ben smiled as he filled the tank, "I guess I am, I've been greasing a car, and that's not a very clean job. I've been trying to call you, Lisa, but you've been so busy, you're hard to find at home. What are your plans after summer, when the pageant is over? Where have you decided to go to school?"

"That depends on the offers that I get after I win the pageant." said Lisa.

"Isn't it a little premature to make your plans around winning?" smiled Ben.

"Why? Don't you think I can win?" she pouted. "And just what are your plans, Ben? Do you expect to work at a gas station all your life?"

Ben smiled good naturedly, "I've been accepted into Pre-Med at UCLA. I'm just working here to help out with the costs of school. I was wondering if you'll be going to school in the L.A. area next year."

"I don't know yet," she said. Embarrassed, and not knowing what to say, she walked around the car. "Put this on Dad's tab."

"OK, Lisa," said Ben, "see you at the pageant."

"I hope he's not making any big plans," she thought to herself. "Ben is a nice boy, but he's only that, a boy."

Lisa put her nose in the air and pulled out of the station. Little finger movements answered Ben's enthusiastic wave. She drove to the shoe store, where she picked up the shoes to match her dress. Next stop was Morgans for the swim suit purchase, before she hurried home.

The next two days were packed with fittings, appointments, and a flurry of luncheons, and practice, practice, practice.

Friday, the day for the pageant dress rehearsal, came at last. Lisa spent a good deal of her time at home with a book on her head. The time seem to fly, and when she looked at the clock, she suddenly realized that she had to be at the pageant hall in forty five minutes.

Lisa showered, did her make-up, and went to her closet to select what to wear. She chose light beige wool gabardine slacks with an ivory silk blouse, topped with a camel's hair jacket. "Don't want my clothes to outshine me," she thought, adding a bright scarf with fall colors on it and a pair of very tailored gold earrings. "Perfect," she mused, Admiring her image in the mirror.

As she hurried out the door, Lisa said to her mother and Nancy, "I should be back by 6:30. If not I'll call. Goodbye you two."

The car started out a little sluggish, but seemed to smooth out as the engine warmed up a bit. She had just about reached the corner where Ben worked when the car started to sputter, chug, and finally stopped altogether. Lisa tried the starter, nothing, she was panic stricken. "They just will not tolerate my being late," she thought. "What'll I do now?" She glanced over at the gas station, and saw Ben coming out of the door of the office. "Ben," she cried, "running toward the station. "My car has just stopped, can you help me get it started? I have to be at the pageant rehearsal in ten minutes."

"Did you say ten minutes?" asked Ben. "You'd better hurry."

"I know," said Lisa, wringing her hands. "Oh Ben, I can't be late."

Ben took over. "We'll call your mom about the car. Your folks can pick it up here later. We'll take my car. I was just getting off work. Come on, it's parked out back."

Lisa looked him up and down, taking in the dirty coveralls, "Well, I guess it's OK, but is your car clean on the inside?"

"Of course," laughed Ben, "I'm not this dirty when I'm not working here, and I want my car just as clean as you do. C'mon, lets go."

They arrived at the auditorium. Lisa hardly waited for Ben to stop the car. She turned to him with a quick "thanks," grabbed her overnight case, and ran.

Ben parked the car, and entered the back of the auditorium. He sat down to wait in case Lisa needed a ride home. He watched the parade of lovely young ladies, comparing them all with Lisa. No doubt about it, in his mind Lisa was the loveliest of all, and in his mind already the winner.

The work crews preparing for the pageant the next day were not finished. They had to finish securing the stairs on the left side of the platform. The girls were practicing coming around the front of the platform and up the stairs on the left. When it was Lisa's turn, typical of Lisa, she put her nose in the air, and started up the stairs She was almost to the top of the make shift stairs when she caught her heel, and tumbled off the stairs on to a stack of stage accessories in wooden crates about ten feet below. There was a frightened cry, and Lisa laid very still.

Everyone looked on in horror, except for Ben. He was out of his seat and to Lisa's side in a heartbeat. He knelt down beside her, and yelled to the crowd standing around. "Someone call an ambulance, please stand back, she's hurt bad."

Ben rode in the ambulance, so that Lisa would not be frightened should she regain consciousness. As soon as they wheeled her into emergency, Ben left her side to call her parents, and they arrived within minutes to wait with Ben for the doctor's appraisal of Lisa's injuries.

All Lisa remembered was a falling sensation, and darkness. Suddenly there was light, and she arrived in an enchantingly beautiful place. She looked around with wonder as she passed through a gate into an incredible garden. She felt very peaceful, happy, and much loved. She sat down on a park bench in the garden and looked around at exotic flowers and plants that she had never seen before. "What a beautiful place this is," thought Lisa. The soft bright light in the garden accented the many shades of pink and lavender which predominated in the garden. The clouds in the sky reflected pink, as though they were made of cotton candy.

Lisa sensed someone near her, and turned her head. She was surprised to see this funny, fancy little man looking at her with curiosity.

"Just who are you, and what are you doing in my garden." he demanded.

"Why, I'm Lisa" she answered, surprised at the question, "And just who are you and what is this lovely place?"

"My name is Fincillet, and you have arrived at my estate on the Island of Corkle."

"Never heard of it," said Lisa.

"Of course you never heard of it," Fincillet said. "You only find it by thinking of it."

"I didn't think of it, so how?... I don't understand." said Lisa.

Fincillet ignored her remark and said "Lisa, Lisa, when will you see what you are doing to yourself?"

"Like what?" said Lisa.

"For one thing," said Fincillet, "Why are you so interested in admiring what is in your mirror. That's only a reflection. The real you, that person that lives in your heart is being neglected."

"So?" said Lisa defensively.

"So how does your best friend like the way you act, and why does she put up with it?" asked Fincillet.

Lisa dropped her gaze," "I don't have a best friend," she answered.

"See what I mean?" said Fincillet.

"Look, I don't need a best friend, I don't need any friends at all. Just what are you getting at?" said Lisa guardedly.

Fincillet looked at her a long minute, and then said, "Lisa, you are very beautiful on the outside. I'm going to give it to you straight. You are not attractive on the inside. You are an unfeeling, ugly, hateful, unlovable witch. You're rude and insensitive to everyone, even those who love you in spite of it all. You are really getting out of hand."

"Look, I don't need any friends," said Lisa, looking down at her feet, "Most people are a waste of time and energy, who needs them?"

"Don't you know that we all need friends? That's just the way the world works. Being number one isn't so great, there are nine numbers in all and they are your support group." said Fincillet. He went on, "We need each other in this world Lisa, and I don't care how unbelievably beautiful you are, you need friends too."

"Why?" asked Lisa.

"Let me ask you this," said Fincillet adjusting the lace at his sleeve, "Lisa, are you happy?"

"Whadda you mean, happy?" asked Lisa, "What are you getting at? Of course I'm happy."

"Don't play games, Lisa," said Fincillet. "Are you content? Just like you are, at this very moment? Are you happy to be who and what you are, or are you lonely?"

Lisa looked down, the tears were welling up in her eyes, and were starting to spill over her lashes to roll down her cheeks, "I can't help being the way I am. I have to try harder to be pretty because I'm not talented. I have to use every trick in the book."

"Do you want to climb that ladder of merit by stepping on everyone's toes, and putting down everybody who gets in your way?" said Fincillet. "The only way you can really be safe is to be yourself. Develop the good things you possess, and there are many. You have talent, Lisa, everyone does, but you have hidden yours away under superficial beauty." Fincillet sat down on the bench beside Lisa and put his bejeweled hand over hers.

"My dear," he began, "we are all special. We all own one thing that works better for us than for anyone else. That's the way the world is designed. Somewhere in that beautiful head of yours is a creative idea that is yours alone. Eventually it will come to you, and you will know it when it does. In the meantime, use kindness, love, and consideration to give it a chance to work. You can't project beauty and love unless you have it there inside yourself."

"Thank you," said Lisa, "I guess I needed that, I seem to feel a lot more comfortable with myself and I'm feeling better now. Wait a minute, I thought I heard someone calling me. Did you hear someone?"

Fincillet looked up and said, "Yes, I heard. It's time for you to go back. Whenever you feel need of encouragement, you know, to be true to yourself, just think of me, I'll be right here. It may seem a little awkward at first, but I expect that in the end we'll become great friends."

Before Lisa walked to the gate and pushed it open, she hugged Fincillet, and said, "Thanks again friend, goodbye" she said.

The doctor had come out of the emergency area into the waiting room. There he saw the anxious faces of Mr. and Mrs. Lindsay, Nancy, and Ben.

"She's going to be OK," he said, "but she has had her right maxillary sinus bones crushed, and there's a severe cut over her right eye, a broken nose, and a broken leg. Really nothing we can't patch, but she will need plastic surgery on her face. You can see her now, but don't stay too long."

They cautiously entered the room. Lisa's leg was in a cast, and her face was covered with bandages. Her lovely eyes looked huge behind the white mask of bandages.

The first face that Lisa recognized was Ben's. "Hi Ben," she whispered.

"Hello beautiful," said Ben.

"Not so beautiful," she replied

"Don't tell me that," smiled Ben.

Lisa talked briefly to her parents, and her little sister. She was sleepy, they had given her something for pain and to make her sleepy. They all left the room feeling much better.

Mrs. Lindsay said, "She's going to be all right. I just want to thank you Ben for everything. I don't know what we would have done without you."

"That's OK, Mrs. Lindsay, you must know by now that Lisa is very special to me."

"We know," she answered with a smile.

Two or three days later Lisa smiled out of her bandaged face. "Hi you two," she said as she saw her mother and sister enter the room. "I was just thinking about you. I forgot to ask in all the excitement, just who won the pageant?"

Nancy and Mrs. Lindsay looked at each other with panic in their eyes. It was the question that they didn't want to answer.

"Mary Turner won dear," Mrs. Lindsay answered softly.

"That's great!" said Lisa to the surprise of them all. "I gave her a terrible time. She really wanted to win as bad as I did. The trouble with me was, I told myself just as I went on-stage to "break a leg" and then I took it to heart," Lisa giggled.

Nancy and Mrs. Lindsay stared at Lisa for a moment. Not believing what they were hearing. Mrs. Lindsay didn't know what to say, so she said "Is there anything you would like us to bring you when we come back?"

"Yes Mom, I would love a chocolate milk shake. Also, would you bring my art supplies, or have Ben bring them, he promised to come by later."

"Will do, dear," said Mrs. Lindsay. "Would you like me to fix your hair?"

"No," said Lisa "I'll just wear it in braids, it'll look O.K., besides, Ben likes me no matter how I look."

TRUNE

Trune is to listen, and that he will do,
He'll perk up his ears and lend them to you.

He'll laugh at your humor or cry at your pain,
A whisper, a shout, to him they're the same.

He knows the impressions that you have inside,
He's tuned to the fact you have feelings you hide.

His antenna will catch the words you can't say,
Go ahead, talk inside, he can hear anyway.

Your dreams of the future he'd sure like to hear,
Your plans for tomorrow, next week, or next year.

"Ambitions," he says, "hold great interest to me,
Confide in me, friend, confidently."

MARTHA AND TRUNE

There was no doubt about it, Martha was really excited about leaving home and getting out into the world. She dreaded the idea of entering into a University where there were so many strangers. Martha was a "loner" in a way, and had very few acquaintances, and only one close friend, Tammy. Tammy had graduated too, but she went on to another school in the Midwest where her grandparents lived.

Martha, the "middle" one in her family, had a big brother five years older, and a little brother six years younger. She was too young to have much of a relationship with her older brother, and too old to enjoy being with her younger brother. She was almost like an only child, as her brothers more or less ignored her. They loved her, but at a distance.

Martha had an uneasy feeling about going away from her family to live on campus in a dorm where she didn't know anyone. "I hope I find someone I can talk to," she thought as she left the airplane and looked around the terminal.

Across the way Martha noticed a sign that read, "Murrysville State University Here." She knew that the school had arranged to meet the Freshmen this first time. Martha picked up her luggage and headed across the terminal to join the others. She joined the group just as a woman was giving directions to the bus waiting outside. Martha couldn't hear the woman clearly, so she asked a girl standing next to her "What is she saying?"

The girl turned and glared at her, "How am I supposed to hear what she is saying with you talking."

Martha stammered, "but I..."

The girl looked directly at her then and said, "Will you please shut up."

"How rude, I guess I'll just have to follow along and see what happens."

They all filed into the waiting bus. Martha held out her I.D. and was directed to a seat in the back. She sat down next to another young woman who acknowledged her with a half smile and a "Hi."

"Hello," answered Martha. "Tell me, do you know how we will be able to find our..." The girl cut her off "My gosh can't you read? It's all in the folder that the school sent to us."

"What folder?" Martha hadn't received any folder from the school. "I didn't get any folder from the school."

The girl looked exasperated, "Why me?" She gathered her things, stood up and moved to another seat.

Martha was squashed. She decided the best thing was to wait for information at the end of the bus trip. Everyone was so "uptight." Martha missed the loving attitude of her parents and Tammy. She thought to herself, "Everyone here acts as though they have a loose nail in their boots. I sure hope that it gets better."

Martha watched as the lovely rural country side passed before her. Then in the distance she could see Murrysville. Stately, covered with ivy, it was a beautiful school. The bus pulled up in front of the first dorm. Just to be sure, the woman in charge announced that she would read off the names as they stopped at each dorm. Martha heard her name called at the third stop , "Martha Dillon."

Martha took her belongings and left the bus. She looked at the building in front of her and thought, "Well this is it." The woman handed Martha her room number as she passed by her. Martha groaned. "Nuts, 206, I'm on the second floor. Oh well, I guess the stairs will do me good!"

When Martha reached the second floor, she found two-zero-six right away. She opened the door and peeked in. One of the rude girls from the bus was sitting at one of the desks. She turned around and glared, "Don't you know enough to knock?"

"I'm sorry, I didn't know anyone was here." Martha looked distressed.

"What did you expect, a private room?" growled the girl. "By the way, I'm Cecila. The bottom bunk is mine."

Martha said nothing. She was close to tears as she checked out the closet. About one forth of the closet was left for her things. Cecila had taken all the rest.

Then Cecila said, "Lets get things straight from the start. I'm not here to be your babysitter. Don't bug me with a bunch of stupid questions."

"Someone has to answer my questions. I know, I'll talk to the dorm mother." Martha thought to herself, as she quickly changed to a pair of slacks and a warm sweater. She turned to look at Cecila, shook her head and left the room without saying a word.

Downstairs Martha found the Dorm Mother's room and knocked gently. "Come in," said a pleasant voice. Martha looked about the cheerful room, and said, "I'm looking for the Dorm Mother."

"You have found her my dear. I'm Ms. Crawford, How can I help?" She smiled at Martha. "Won't you sit down, er what is your name?"

"My name is Martha Dillon. I hear I was supposed to have a orientation folder, but it didn't arrive before I left to come here. It was late, or I was overlooked, I was wondering if I could get another folder from you."

"Of course. We're here to help all we can. Supper is at 5:30, which is in ten minutes. Maybe you could come back later and talk. Here's your folder, look it over and see if you have any questions I can answer for you." Ms. Crawford smiled, Martha thought to herself, "Hooray, a good guy"

Martha left Ms. Crawford's room and looked up the directions to the dining room. When she arrived at the cafeteria building she entered and the wonderful smell of food hit her nose. She saw Cecila, but went out of her way to avoid her, and sat down at a table on the other side of the room. She thumbed through her folder while she began to eat her supper. Suddenly she was aware of someone at her elbow. "OK if I sit down?"

Martha looked up into a very pleasant round face. "Of course, let me move some of this stuff. Then she said, "I'm Martha Dillon, and live in the Evergreens dorm." She smiled as she added, "You're the first friendly face I've seen outside of my dorm mother. Please, sit down."

The girl grinned at Martha. "I'm Abbie Perkins. I live over at the other side of the campus in the Woodside dorm. I know what you mean about unfriendly. What's wrong with people anyway?"

"Who knows," said Martha. "Tell me is this your first year?"

"Sort of," answered Abbie, "I had to drop out in January of last year. I had an asthma attack."

"That's too bad" Martha sympathized, "I hope all goes better with you this time, I would like to be friends."

"Thanks Martha, me too."

Martha and Abbie discussed their studies and their schedules. They had no classes or other scheduled events together, but they decided they would get together when they could, and maybe see about changing their schedules next semester.

The time passed, Abbie and Martha had become good friends. Although they had nothing scheduled together they managed to meet at the library, or the student union just to talk. One day Martha and Abbie had arranged to meet so they could attend a football rally together. Martha waited, and when Abbie didn't show up Martha went to her dorm to find out why.

One of the girls in Abbie's dorm was just coming out the door.

Martha asked, "Where's Abbie, she was supposed to meet me and go to the rally."

"They came and got her," said the girl. "She had another bad asthma attack and there wasn't time for her to say goodbye to anyone."

Martha was stricken. "Oh no, poor Abbie, who will I talk to?" Martha broke into sobs and ran toward her own dorm. "The only friend I have... gone. Oh Abbie I will miss you dreadfully. Who will listen, Who will care like you have? " she sobbed.

It was a beautiful spring day and Martha paused to catch her breath. She leaned against the tree and cried. "Abbie was my only real friend on campus. Now she's gone, I have no one, to share things with."

"You have me," said a voice so close Martha jumped with surprise.

"Wha....?" she looked in the crook of the tree and there sat a funny little man with enormous ears and a hearing trumpet. "I will listen Martha. I will listen to your plans, your dreams, the feelings you hide I can hear too. Please don't cry, I'll be here for you." he said.

"But who are you? Where do you come from? How do you know about me?" Martha dumped all the questions at once.

"I'm Trune" said the little man. "I listen to those who need some one to listen, to be there, to plan with." Trune smiled, "I'm a real friend."

Martha could not believe her eyes and ears It didn't matter to her that this was all fantasy, it was just what she needed. She sank down on the grass. Clasping her hands together, she said, "Oh Trune, if you are what you say you are I can sure use you for a friend."

"What's been happening Martha? What do we need to do specifically?"

First of all," said Martha, "there's this room mate of mine. She walks all over me."

"Why do you let her do that?" replied Trune. She can walk all over you only if you lie down and take it. By not being assertive you are allowing her to push you around."

"I never thought of it that way," said Martha. That's why I don't have many friends except for Abbie, and now she's gone."

"Why do you suppose that is?" asked Trune.

"Probably because I'm afraid. Afraid that they'll answer me like

Cecila does," answered Martha.

"Cecila sounds to me like an angry girl," said Trune. "I wonder what hurt feelings she has for her to be so unpleasant."

"Who cares!" said Martha.

"Oh Martha, we must care about each other. Don't you know we're all in this world together?" said Trune.

Martha paused for a moment. Two boys were walking nearby. She didn't want them to think she was sitting there talking to a tree.

"Wait," she whispered to Trune, "can those boys see you Trune?" she asked.

"No, only you can see me," said Trune "I'm only seen by whomever I want to be seen."

Martha watched apprehensively as the two walked on across the campus, never even noticing she was there. "You're right of course, about caring I mean, but Cecila can be so impossible."

"Probably the very reason you need to become her friend," said Trune.

"What do you mean?" asked Martha, "Cecila would never let me become her friend."

"Cecila will become your friend when you are strong enough to handle the friendship. She walks all over you, Martha, because she knows she can get away with it," said Trune "You're going to let her know she can't do this any more."

"I am?" answered Martha.

"You are," said Trune. "You'll see her soften up and become closer to you. You'll see. Cecila needs someone strong. You can help Cecila and yourself at the same time by being stronger. Change things Martha. How about starting with a speech class?"

"Why a speech class?"

"A speech class will help you talk in front of others. It'll give you confidence in yourself. You'll learn sentence skills and poise, just to mention a couple of things. Sign up for a class in Psychology that will cover assertive behavior, you'll change, you won't be able to stop a change."

"I guess it's worth a try," said Martha.

"No guessing about it," said Trune. "Gotta go now. Someone else needs me. Do it Martha. Start now. I'll get back to you."

Martha watched flabbergasted as Trune simply disappeared and Martha was left alone. Martha said to herself, "Was he real? Never mind, what he said was real that's for sure."

When Martha got back to the dorm she headed for Ms. Crawford's office. Once there she told Ms. Crawford about her decision to change a couple of classes. Ms. Crawford seemed to think too that a speech class and a course in assertiveness would be very good for Martha. Martha thanked Ms. Crawford for her help, turned, and ran upstairs.

Martha paused at the door of room two-zero-six, pulled in her breath and knocked softly.

"Yeah, who is it?" said Cecila.

"It's me," answered Martha.

"Oh you, well come on in," said Cecila, not looking up.

Martha entered the room, walked over to the closet to hang up her coat. She found there was not enough room.

"Cecila," she said, "you're going to have to make room in the closet. I don't even have enough room to hang up my coat."

Cecila turned around. Her mouth was hanging open. "You can't be serious," she said. "I have no intention of moving anything."

"I'm very serious," said Martha. "You don't wear half of the things in there, and they could easily be packed carefully in a box that would slide under the bunks. That's what I have had to do."

"I'm not moving a thing" said Cecila

"You move them or I will!" said Martha.

"You'd better not touch my things." warned Cecila.

"Or you'll do what?" said Martha.

"I'll, I'll report you," replied Cecila getting red now with anger and frustration.

"Report me for taking my half of the closet?" Martha snickered, "I don't think so. Please have things changed by the time I return."

"Or?" said Cecila.

"Or you just might find your things on the floor," said Martha. She left the room struggling to keep her face straight. Trune was right. Cecila needs someone strong. When Martha got back from supper, Cecila had made room for Martha. The closet was straightened, and was more organized.

When Martha went to hang up her coat, she noticed there was plenty of room for her now. She said "Thanks Cecila, I mean it, the closet really looks nice."

"Umph." answered Cecila.

Martha turned then and smiled. "By the way, Cecila, I didn't see you over at supper. I know how you love chocolate chip cookies. There were only a few left, and I knew that by the time you got over there they'd be all gone, so I grabbed some for you."

"You did?" Cecila asked with surprise. "Gee, Martha, thanks."

"No problem," replied Martha. That was the beginning.

Martha's speech class was a big help. At first the thought of standing up in front the class terrified her, but when she mentioned it to Trune he said, "Just look out there and imagine a garden with rows and rows of cabbage heads. Now who's afraid of cabbages?" Martha laughed every time she thought of being fearful. She got better at speaking, and was getting good grades for her written speeches. Martha found herself speaking out more and more.

Martha met Trune frequently at the tree to talk things over. He was most enthusiastic with her progress. He was happy that Cecila was beginning to come around too.

Then there was the psychology class that dealt with assertive behavior and the building of self esteem. Martha's new-found personality, along with her sweet, pleasant nature, made her a dynamite person. Martha was beginning to make many new friends, but Cecila was her "project" and the two of them were getting close, very close.

One afternoon Martha and Cecila were talking and the subject of their first few weeks came up.

"Will you please explain to me just what you were so disturbed about," said Martha.

Cecila hesitated, "Just before I left for school my parents separated. "I hated everyone and everything."

"How terrible., said Martha. "No wonder you were hurting. How are things now?"

"No better, no worse," said Cecila. "'Thanks for putting up with me, Martha."

"A very good friend of mine told me once that we must care about each other," said Martha. "I must say, at first you weren't too lovable."

"And you were wimpy," said Cecila laughing. "I guess we were lucky to find each other."

One afternoon Martha sat down beside the special tree. She was daydreaming a little, thinking of all the things that had come to pass. She heard a rustle of leaves and turned around to see Trune grinning at her.

"Martha, my friend, it's time for me to move on. You're doing fine. You and Cecila are caring for each other," said Trune.

"Won't I see you again?" asked Martha.

"Probably not, you don't really need me now that you have Cecila. Besides, you've made a lot of new friends in your speech class. You've become sort of a 'Trune' yourself in showing people you care about what they have to say, and what they need to express," said Trune.

"Where will you go now?" asked Martha.

"There's a married couple who are separated," said Trune. "I'm going to show them how much they need to listen to each other. I'll remind them that caring is what it is all about."

"I didn't know you did couples," said Martha." You know, Cecila's parents separated and ....."

Trune interrupted, "I leave you with this: Do learn to listen, too. That little voice in your head that says 'do it'.....or 'don't do it' is your friend. Be sure to listen carefully!"

LURKIT

Because he is Lurkit, he'll cheat and he'll lie,
He sneaks and he slinks and he acts very sly.

Imposter he is, a rogue and a faker,
His number one job is misery maker.

He knows that deception is never all right,
By being deceitful he keeps your crown bright.

His cape of protection will keep you away,
From things you might do to darken your day.

Let Lurkit take over the fraud that might tempt you,
Since Lurkit is crooked, his acts will exempt you.

Now add up the things you know you ought not,
Lurkit will do them so you won't get caught.

EDDIE AND LURKIT

Eddie watched his mother as she busied herself getting ready to leave for work. She always packed a lunch, a magazine or newspaper, and emergency things "just in case." She readied Eddie's supper and put out the things for Arnie too. Eddie's father was due home soon, but there would be a couple of hours when Eddie and his little brother would be alone.

"I hate to see you go out tonight, Mom," said Eddie. "It's going to be cold and it looks like snow." He watched as his mother put on a heavy coat. It was not the best weather to be out in, and he always worried about his mother working at night.

"Well son, I hate to go, but we need the extra money. Your father works hard, but he can't do it all, we all have to help out. If you hate to see me go, remember I need you to be a good boy and watch over your little brother, and stay away from those bums downstairs."

"They're not so bad Mom, at least they have each other to hang around with. I'm always home alone with Arnie" Eddie couldn't look directly at his mother, he knew how his parents felt about the gang of young boys who wasted their time hanging around the steps on the front of the building just looking for trouble, or making trouble of their own. "Really some of them are real cool guys," said Eddie.

"I imagine they are 'cool.' The way they wear their father's pants that flap around their legs in the wind, I'd be cool too," said Mrs. Pattrino.

"You know what I mean Mom. They have fun together," said Eddie.

"Their kind of fun you don't need, Eddie," said his mother. "Eddie, we're a family, we need each other. I do my work, your Dad does his, and your job is getting good grades in school and watching out for

Arnie. If you want to join a gang, go to the YMCA or the Boy's Club, or join the Gym Rats at St. Andrew's. Look, I gotta go or I'll miss my bus. Just remember, those so-called "cool" members of our neighborhood downstairs are an accident waiting to happen, and like I said, don't stay out after dark, lock the door, and be good to Arnie." With that she kissed Eddie and his little brother lightly, and was out the door and down the stairs.

"Bye, Mom," said Eddie. He heard Arnie in the other room watching his cartoons. "He's a good little guy," thought Eddie. He peeked in to see if he was OK and if he needed anything. Then he looked around. His schoolbooks were waiting for him on the kitchen table. Eddie sat down to begin his studies.

Eddie was halfway into his history assignment when he heard something hit the window. "What?" He got up and walked over to see what was going on. There below was the familiar group that hung around the outside stairs. He opened the window and looked out. "What's going on?" he asked. "Whadda you guys want?"

"C'mon down," answered Bernie, one of the group below.

"Can't do that guys, I have to do my homework, and watch out for my little brother like I always do," said Eddie.

"Oh, what a good boy you are," jeered another member of the gathering. "Are you afraid your ol' lady and ol' man will get ticked off? If they do, so what? C'mon down for just a minute. What are you, a man or a mouse?"

Eddie was bored, and he was curious. Why would they suddenly be interested in him, he wondered. He glanced in at Arnie, "Hey, Arnie I'm going downstairs for a while."

Arnie looked up. "You're not supposed to. Dad won't like it."

"I'm going. Lock the door after me Arnie," said Eddie. He went out the door and down the stairs.

Eddie was surrounded as he came down the steps. There were six of them. They called themselves "The Animals." They had all shaved their heads, or had haircuts that were fashioned to leave very little hair on their heads. To be sure they resembled animals, but what kind? Eddie wasn't sure. One of them carried a tape-recorder-radio that they referred to as a "ghetto blaster." The sound that was coming from it was the kind of rock that Eddie's mother would have said "kills your plants."

Eddie was a little uncomfortable being surrounded, but they were all very congenial, and soon he was put at ease and began to relax a little.

"Hey Eddie," said the one they called "Cat," "Eddie, we ah, want you to, ah, join our gang."

Eddie looked surprised and uneasy. "Whadda you mean, what do I have to do? Why would you want me? I don't think my mom and dad would—."

Cat cut him off. "Listen man, you don't live your life for your ol' lady or your ol' man do you?"

"Well, I—-," stammered Eddie, not wanting to irritate the group.

"First of all," said "Halo", another of the circled youths, "First of all you have to do an initiation. We need fifty bucks. You're going to get it for us."

"How can I do that? That's impossible," said Eddie. "I don't have a job, and I don't have any money." Now Eddie realized why they had called him downstairs.

"Doesn't your ol' lady keep some money in the house for house-hold stuff?" asked Cat

"I can't touch that," said Eddie before he realized that he shouldn't have said anything at all.

"Why not?" asked Halo, "she'll never know."

"Yes she would," said Eddie. "She counts every penny. Besides, if I were to take the money, how could I ever pay it back?"

"We get little errand jobs, Eddie, delivering stuff for the big guys uptown. We'll give you a couple of these jobs to cover the fifty. You can make fifty bucks just making one delivery." Cat made it sound simple.

"If I don't join?" asked Eddie, almost in a whisper.

"Then you're the enemy," roared a voice behind him. Eddie whirled around to face "The Fist."

"If you're not one of the gang, then we'd naturally have to protect ourselves against you, and your little brother," said the gang member.

Eddie felt his blood run cold. He was trapped and there didn't seem to be much he could do about it.

That was the beginning. The original $50.00 he took from the teapot in the kitchen was put back after Eddie had made several "drops" for what he came to know as "the guys uptown." He became more and more involved and even started leaving Arnie alone while he "hung out" with the gang members. Sometimes they cruised around and spray painted any surface they found blank. Other times they had minor skirmishes with other gangs or the police. They would surround and intimidate unsuspecting members of the community just for fun. It made them feel powerful and important.

Eddie was always home when his father got home. Then he pretended to go to bed, and as soon as it was quiet he'd sneak out his window and down the fire escape to join the others. He didn't like the idea of deceiving his parents, but he was fourteen, and Eddie felt he had a "right" to some friends, and some fun.

Most of the gang members were into drugs. Eddie didn't like the taste nor the sensation that drugs gave him. For that reason he became an important member of the group. He could be depended on to have his wits about him at all times. He became their lookout.

Mr. and Mrs. Pattrino became more and more puzzled at the behavior of their son. He had always been more "open" with them. He had become sullen, and was more to himself. He had gotten a haircut that Mrs. Pattrino referred to as a fuzzy onion.

There was a group of seven boys, counting Eddie, and they always dressed in a strange manner. They had slogans on their clothing. If they wore hats, they were baseball caps, usually worn backwards with white lettering on the back or the sides of the hat.

Eddie had been called into the office at school several times for being in fights, and for "bothering" straight students. His teachers were troubled too, as he had really changed. His grades had taken a nosedive, and his usual polite attitude had changed . He had become rude and unruly. He changed his "straight" dress after his parents left, and he wore the bizarre dress of the group to school. "At least I'm not bored," he thought to himself one day, "and I have friends, such as they are."

But Eddie was not happy. He was into a whole lifestyle that was impossible to get out of and that he was unhappy being in. Every time he'd ask about leaving the gang he was met by terrifying threats against him or his family. And so it went on until.......

Eddie had left Arnie in front of the TV, or at least he thought he had. He had gone downstairs to the front steps to join the gang. What he didn't know was that Arnie had become bored too, and had followed him downstairs to stand in the shadows of the front doorway behind them. He just wanted to be near his brother.

The gang had gathered on the bottom step of the stairs, some were sitting, some leaning against the railing. They were just having a "rap" session, discussing their plans for the evening. All of a sudden around the corner down the block came a low black sedan full of guys Eddie had never seen before. As the car drove by the place where Eddie and the group were congregated, there was a sudden crack, crack, crack noise, and one of Eddie's gang yelled "get down, get down." The car accelerated and flew down the street and around the corner. When the car disappeared they looked around and saw that two of the gang had been shot!

"I'll call for some medics," yelled Eddie and started up the steps. Just inside the doorway he stumbled over something. He looked down and saw the small crumpled body of his little brother. Arnie was hit in the chest and was bleeding badly. "Oh my God," said Eddie, and the tears nearly blinded him as he ran upstairs to the phone. After talking quickly to 911 Eddie ran downstairs to his brother's side. He took Arnie into his arms to comfort him.

Mr. Pattrino was walking down his street from his bus stop. He looked startled when he heard the sirens, and then he started running when he saw that the police were arriving in front of his building. He watched as a couple of ambulances pulled up at his address. When he got there he looked around and passed by the fallen boys on the steps. He stopped horrified at the top of the steps. He looked into the doorway and saw Eddie holding the limp little body of his younger brother. Eddie's tears streaked face. Looking up at his father he said, "He's hurt pretty bad dad."

Mr. Pattrino turned around and yelled at the paramedics. "Over here, over here." Then he looked at Eddie with fury and said, "Is this the way you take care of your little brother? Here! Give him to me!"

Mr. Pattrino took Arnie's quiet body into his arms and carried him outside. He gently handed him to the paramedics. They put the injured little boy on a stretcher and checked out his vital signs.

"He's alive," said one of the medics, "but just barely." He asked Mr. Pattrino, "Are you his father?"

Mr. Pattrino nodded.

"Come on, you had better go with us," said the Medic. Mr. Pattrino followed him and they both disappeared into the ambulance. The doors shut and Eddie heard someone say, "General Hospital, 7th and Champion, and hurry."

Eddie collapsed and sat down on the steps. He buried his head in his arms and sobbed. "Arnie, oh Arnie, I'm, so sorry." He didn't notice the rest of the activity. The police and the medics took the two gang members to the hospital, and the rest of the gang just stood around. Eddie's mind was filled with pictures of his happy-go-lucky little innocent brother covered with blood, lying there so still and white.

Suddenly Eddie heard someone call his name.

"Eddie, hey, Eddie." He looked up and saw "Halo" and "Cat." Hey man, whadda ya doing slobbering about your brother? He'll probably make it OK."

Eddie saw red. "Probably?" he shouted. "Whadda you mean probably?" Eddie jumped to his feet, and with power he didn't know he had he grabbed the "Cat" and whirled him around. Then, reaching over the fence rail he hit him squarely in the face. He saw "Halo" coming for him and he slugged him as hard as he could. Eddie watched with no regret as he saw "Halo " roll down the steps to the sidewalk.

Eddie dusted himself off and started down the street toward the hospital. He was unaware of the tears rolling down his face, or his bloodied clothes.

A patrol car came up alongside Eddie and asked. "Wasn't that little guy that got shot your brother?" Eddie looked at him and nodded. The officer then asked "Would you like a lift?" Eddie managed a weak smile.

"I'm going to the hospital," he said.

"Hop in kid, I'll take you" said the officer. General Hospital was a big place. The officer who took Eddie with him luckily knew his way around. He took Eddie to the emergency entrance and let him off there. "Thanks," yelled Eddie, as he watched the officer drive away.

Eddie ran up the steps, directed by the large lighted arrow that read **EMERGENCY**. "Scary, very scary," thought Eddie. He slowly pushed open the door and almost tiptoed into the area. He saw his father sitting with his big hands covering his face. His mother had come. She looked gray. She stood leaning against a windowsill looking out into the night at nothing. She saw only the image of her younger son before they had wheeled him into surgery.

Eddie cautiously entered the room. His mother saw him first. "Is this the way you care for your baby brother?" She sobbed, "Oh Eddie, how could you?"

Mr. Pattrino looked up and shouted, "Get out of my sight!"

Eddie, tears streaming down his face, said "I'll wait outside." He left and went out the back way. He sat down close to the big drain from the hospital purification plant. He hugged his knees and looked gloomily into the night.

"Hey you." Eddie looked around him. He heard the voice, but he didn't see anyone. "Hey crumb bum." The sound seemed to be coming from the big drain pipe just below him. Eddie got up and moved closer, then he saw it—-him—-whatever it was. It looked sorta like an alligator, but sorta human too.

"Who me?" Eddie asked. "Did you speak to me? If so, who are you to be calling me a crumb bum?"

"Yes, you." answered the creature. "Just look what you have done to your family."

Eddie hung his head. "Who are you anyway, and what makes you think that this is any of your business?"

"I'm Lurkit, and I'm making it my business for your own good." he said.

"Why? And just what's a Lurkit? And where do you come from?"

"You saw," said Lurkit. "I came out of that drain. I came to help you before you mess up your life any further. That's what I do. If a guy like you wants to get out of a gang or situation, or whatever mess, I take over their crime wave."

"Oh give me a break," said Eddie. "How could you expect to do that?"

"Because," said Lurkit, "I'm what's known as a "Fantasy." I can do anything you imagine I can."

"You mean you're not real?" asked Eddie.

"I'm real all right," answered Lurkit. "I take over the dark or evil thoughts that you might have so that your mental coast is clear. Get the idea?"

"Kinda, but just how does it work?"

"You'll see," said Lurkit. "Just ask me to get rid of the dark or bad side of your thoughts and I'll do it. I do all the bad stuff that you might get into for you so that you can remain the good kid I know you are."

"That's great for you to say, but it's too late. Look what has happened to Arnie. It's all my fault. I wouldn't blame my folks if they never talked to me again." said Eddie. "How can my parents ever forgive me?"

"Your mom and dad are very frightened right now, Eddie. By the way, Arnie is going to be OK. Your folks just want the best for you and Arnie.

They want to see you grow up and have a happy life, a better one than they've had. It breaks their hearts to see that you have changed into a bum. It's getting cold out here," go on back in and wait with your parents. The doctors are just now finishing up. Go on now."

"Thanks for everything," said Eddie. "How will I get in touch with you again?"

"The next time a bad situation comes up, just think of me, and call "Lurkit" and I'll step right in to take the fraud that might tempt you. First thing you know you'll be squeaky clean." Lurkit turned then, and before Eddie could say anymore, he slithered away and disappeared into the drain pipe.

"I imagined all that and it sure was nuts," said Eddie to no one in particular, "but it did make me feel better. Lurkit is right, my folks do want what's right for me. I know it was just a fantasy and all that, but it was so real, and it did make me feel better."

Eddie slowly went up the steps and into the emergency waiting room. His mom and dad were still waiting anxiously. They didn't even look up when Eddie entered the room. Eddie sat down quietly to wait there with them.

All of a sudden the big double doors into the operating room were pushed open.

The doctor looked at Eddie's folks. "You are Mr. and Mrs. Pattrino?" He could tell by their anxious expression they were the boy's parents.

"Yes," said Mr. Pattrino.

"Arnie," cried Mrs. Pattrino, "how's my baby?"

"Well," said the doctor, "he's had a very close call. He was shot twice, but luckily, nothing vital was damaged. He's lost a lot of blood, but he's going to make it. We'll need to keep him here a week or two, but you can visit as much as you like." The doctor turned to Eddie. "You must be Eddie."

Eddie nodded. The doctor went on. "Arnie asked for you. He wants to see you. You must be a wonderful brother, he loves you very much. But he is asleep now so you'll have to wait until tomorrow morning."

The doctor's words cut into Eddie like a knife. He leaned against the wall and sobbed. All at once he felt his Dad's arms around him, and he turned around to see his dad's forgiving smile. They all hugged each other at once and cried with joy. Arnie was going to be OK!

Mr. Pattrino looked at his watch. It was almost eleven o'clock. He said to Eddie and his wife, "You know, I'm suddenly very hungry. how about you two?" Eddie and his Mom agreed.

While they ate at the neighborhood diner, Eddie explained what had happened. He explained how he got tricked into joining in the first place, and how the gang threatened him if he talked about leaving. He explained to his parents how scared he was. Then he said, there was nothing they could do that would hurt him any more than what had happened to Arnie. "They were responsible," said Eddie. "I will never ever forget that!"

They talked things through that night as the three of them walked slowly home together. Mr. Pattrino vowed to stick close to Eddie to help him overcome the gang's threats. He also said that they would make plans to move to another area, so that Eddie could make a new start.

Three nights later Mr. Pattrino came home excited and very happy. "It's gonna happen, Eddie, I got a great job offer with much more money in a neighborhood across town. There's a nice apartment that comes with it. Your mom won't have to work, and you'll be able to join the Y or the Boy's Club. I want you to learn the martial arts so that you can take care of yourself."

Eddie and his father sat down with their hot chocolate and cookies to wait for Eddie's mom to come home. They couldn't wait to tell her the good news. They'd be moved in and settled before Arnie got home.

Eddie did speak to Lurkit again. They became, in fact, very good friends. A couple of times Eddie sent Lurkit to his friends that were almost in trouble. Eddie went on to live a lifestyle that his parents were very proud of. Arnie found him to be a wonderful role model and a very happy big brother.

GRATCHET

Gratchet's the bird that has nerve to spare,
To help you do things that you wouldn't dare.

When your tongue's in a knot, and you're shy in a crowd,
Are you crying inside while you're smiling out loud?

He'll spread out his wings and help you to fly,
He helps you keep smiling when you want to cry.

Are you lacking the courage to tackle the task?
Then just summon Gratchet, that's all you need ask.

He'll teach you the lesson to try is to do,
And direct you to use the best that is you.

He's just what you need, a "can do it" man,
And you'll do great things, 'cause he says you can.

TIM AND GRATCHET

Tim kicked at the small rocks and dirt clods in his path as he made his way home from school. His hands thrust deep in his pockets, his head down, his face clouded, his anger and frustration were really showing as he walked along.

"I knew I wouldn't make the football team," he thought." I'm too little, I'm not strong enough, I'm too slow, and besides, I don't like contact sports. Dad will be disappointed, he was so good at sports. Mom will be her own "You're wonderful Timmy" self. They just don't understand, I'm only me, just ol' Tim Anders, not good enough for anything."

Tim shuffled his way home, slowly putting one foot in front of the other. Fighting back the tears, he went up the steps to the front door and tried the latch. He rattled the doorknob. "Locked," he thought, "they must be around back in the garden."

With a heavy heart Tim went around to the back yard. There they were in deep conversation at the table under the umbrella. Tim stood quietly for a moment and looked at them, and suddenly he realized how much he loved them both and how much he wanted their approval.

"I'm one lucky kid to have them for parents," he thought.

At the sound of Tim's step his parents looked up and smiled . "Hi, Timmy," said his mother, "would you like some lemonade?"

"No thanks, Mom," Tim smiled and looked toward his Dad.

"How did your team trials go, son?" said his father.

"Terrible, Dad," Tim's heart sank when he saw his father's disappointed face. "I was awful, they nearly killed me!"

"Never mind, Tim, " said his Dad, "there is always another time, right?"

Tim managed a weak smile and said, "yeah, right Dad". With a lump in his throat Tim looked at the two of them, and said "If you two don't mind, I think I'll go up and study a little before supper, OK?"

"You go on Timmy," said his mother, "supper won't be ready for another hour or so."

Tim opened the back door and headed up the back stairs. "I'm sure glad that's over with," he thought. "I hated to have to tell them." Tim opened the door to his bedroom and looked around. "Home safe" he thought.

Tim's bedroom looked familiar and comfortable. There were the clean folded clothes his mother had put on his bed to put away. He stacked a couple of books on his night stand, took his clean clothes and put them away. "This is my room," he thought, "my place, my warm welcome safe haven."

His big bed beckoned and he headed for its security. He sat down, lay back, and just let his body sink into the bed's soft surrounding comfort. He finally felt his body start to relax.

Tim reached for a book on the night stand. He thumbed through a few pages and attempted to do some reading. His mind was still too full of hurt and disappointment. "Dad really was counting on me to make the team," he thought. "I did try, but to be honest, not too hard. I was really glad when I didn't make it. The only thing is, I've let Dad down. He doesn't realize that I don't like contact sports, that I would really rather play tennis. There! I said it."

Tim let the sad thoughts roll around in his head. He laid the book aside, "I can't concentrate," he decided, "lately I can't do anything right. I'm scared I won't ever be someone to be proud of."

The relaxing comfort of the bed was making Tim feel sleepy. All the happenings of the day were suddenly exhausting. After laying the book back on the table, Tim started to drift off. Just as he was almost asleep, he felt a thump-bump on the end of the bed.

Tim looked up startled, rubbed his eyes and was surprised to see a bird perched on the end of his bed. "What?" He sat up. It was not only a bird, but a large blue bird with an Aussie "outback" hat, and a belt with "can-do" written on it's buckle. "This is unreal" he thought to himself, and yet there it was, big as life.

"Where did you come from?" asked Tim. Then he thought, "This is nuts. Birds can't answer me, and they sure don't wear hats and belts."

Suddenly the bird hopped across the end of the bed, cocked it's head, and looked at Tim with one eye. Then a big smile spread across his beak. "I came in from the window just now. But I originally flew in from the Island of Corkle. But, that's not important. What is important is that you are not happy. You're a first class sad sack my friend, and it's really all your own fault. You need to clean up your depressing act. By the way, my name is Gratchet."

"Wait just a large darn minute," said Tim. "Whadda you mean, it's all my fault? You don't know what you're talking about. I can't be all the things that Mom and Dad want me to be. I can't." Tim's eyes filled with angry tears.

"So don't try," said Gratchet. "Don't try to be anyone but yourself, understand? It's not what others expect from you that's important, it's what you expect from yourself. I'm not saying you should not respect your parents, but for heaven's sake have a little respect for yourself. You're the one you have to live with."

Gratchet cocked his head and looked Tim right in the eye, "Get the idea? You're not a failure, you are someone very special. See, ya' gotta pour energy into your own specialty to make it great. Understand?

"Sorta," said Tim.

"Let me put it this way," said Gratchet. "What you've gotta do is put aside the 'yeah-buts', and cancel the 'I can'ts', and establish in your head what you want, and then go for it. Just begin. Look Tim, nobody shows us birds where to fly south. We begin, take to the air, and just go. Get the idea?"

"Mom and Dad wouldn't understand," said Tim. "They have their big plans for me."

"Tim, your parents are a lot more understanding than you give them credit for. Let them know that you have big plans and dreams yourself. Have you ever told them how you feel?"

"No," said Tim, "I was afraid to. They seem so set on what they want me to do."

"That's just it," said Gratchet. "It's what they want you to do. You have to level with them. I betcha they'll be happy that you've given your future some thought yourself. They are going to be proud of you, no matter how you achieve success as long as you do it honestly. You have to put your best foot forward, then your next best foot. Reach out and grab a handful of the world. Dare to do the best you can do. Charge your inner batteries with positive thoughts like, 'I can,' 'I will,' 'I'm very good at what I do'." Gratchet was really getting into it, jumping up and down and squawking along with talking.. "Look Tim, so you're not perfect yet, life isn't that easy. Nobody becomes perfect overnight. Right now if you feel less than perfect, 'wing it' that's what we birds do, at least you can fly in the meantime. Get it?"

"Where do I start?" asked Tim. He was starting to get excited and very interested.

"Lay the groundwork, Tim," said Gratchet. "Establish your goals, the little ones, and the big ones. Start right where you are. First tell your parents how you feel, and then you can go for it. Practice, try again if things don't work, try again, try again, don't EVER give up. Look at Thomas Edison he had a lot more failures than he did successes." Gratchet was hopping up and down waving his wings like a cheer leader.

"OK, bird, all that's great, but where do I begin?" said Tim.

"Begin," said Gratchet "by striving to be the best you can be. Greatness is in everybody, but you don't get it free, you have to work for it. Start studying all the subjects that will take you toward your goals." "Do you mean study my school class material?" asked Tim.

"Right," said Gratchet, "you can't reach goals without knowledge, Once your classes are going well you can take time to give some serious thought to your tennis game, if that's what you want to do. Read about the tennis 'Greats' and how they play the game. In all things be the best you can be. Stop the 'inner whimpering",said Gratchet. "If you feel sorry for yourself you need to fix the things that make you feel inferior. Dare to be the wonderful person you have locked inside yourself, and for heaven's sake untie the knots in your tongue."

Tim looked at Gratchet long and hard. "I will honestly try, but if things don't work out, how do I get in touch with you?" asked Tim.

"You don't have to get in touch with me, I'll be in touch with you." Gratchet said. Then he smiled at Tim. "I found you in the first place, right?"

"Right," said Tim.

"I have to go now, Tim. Remember all I have told you." Gratchet then whirled around and before Tim could stop him, flew right out the window.

Tim lay back on his bed and slowly went over all the things Gratchet had said. "There's a lot going for that bird." he thought. "Now, wait a minute. Was that bird for real? I must have been dreaming. Wow, what a great dream! Wish I could dream like that all the time. Yeah, that was it, I was dreaming." Tim got up from his bed, as he heard his mother call for supper. He went in to wash his hands and dry them. When Tim looked back at his bed he saw something on his pillow. "What is that?" he wondered. He went over to his bed to look closer. It was a feather. A blue feather. "Wow, that's cool." Tim whispered to himself as looked pensively out the window. He left his room and went downstairs to supper with a big warm smile on his face.

Mr. Anders looked up as Tim came into the living room. "Did you have a good study, son?" he asked Tim.

"I guess I dozed off, Dad, I sure didn't get much studying done."

"Well, you most likely needed the nap, Timmy," said his Mom as she poked her head into the living room. "Come on you two, supper is on the table."

Tim's mind was still whirling from his encounter with Gratchet. He was silently wondering yet if it was a dream, or something weird in his imagination. His Dad looked at him and said.

"Is there something you'd like to tell us, Tim? You look as though you have something important on your mind."

Tim looked at his Dad, and then at his mother. "I had a funny dream, there was this bird..." Tim shook his head. "You know," he said, "I guess it was a dream, or it had to be, I mean, did I imagine the whole thing?"

"Why don't you tell us about it, Tim," said his father. "It sounds like it ought to be interesting."

"Well, I know this is going to sound stupid, but there I was resting on my bed, sorta laid back relaxed, and this bird flew in my window."

"Flew in your window? A bird?" his mother exclaimed.

"Yeah," said Tim. "He sat right down on the end of my bed with a thump, and then hopped around telling me all the things that are wrong with me, and told me how to start changing." His parents looked at each other questioningly.

Tim went on, "He was blue, and he had on a hat, you know the kind that they wear in the Australian outback? And he had on a belt too. It was kinda shiny, and it had 'can do' written on it. Don't think that I'm crazy, but he talked to me—about winning and losing, about, excuse me, Mom, but about having the guts to be myself and go for my own dreams. You know what I mean? That kind of stuff."

Tim looked at them both. "He told me that I had to talk to the two of you about my future, and that you would understand."

Tim's parents looked at him, then at each other. His mother, uncomfortable with the whole subject, said, "Let's start supper before things get cold." She was puzzled with the idea of a bird in his room that could talk, and who wore a hat and a belt. "You'll feel better with a good hot supper in your tummy," she said.

Tim thought to himself, "Mom's answer to everything, a little tender loving care, and lots of good food. It would cure anything."

As they seated themselves around the table, there was a sort of unsettling quiet pause as they all looked at each other. Mr. Anders finally looked directly at Tim and said, "What do you think all this means, Tim?" He reached for the mashed potatoes all the while looking right at his son. "Potatoes, Tim?"

Tim helped himself as he looked alternately from one parent to the other, then to the spoon in his hand. "I don't know for sure the meaning of it all, Dad, but it sure did make me feel better. Gratchet, that's the bird's name," said Tim. "Gratchet helped me a little to understand that you really wanted me to be on the team. But you see, I'm not you, I'm me, and I don't like to play football. I don't like to play any contact sports. Would you really want me to play just for you and not for myself?" Tim looked down, almost afraid to look at his Dad.

Mr. Anders looked bewildered. "You mean that you were doing all that just for me? Oh Tim, for me?" Tim nodded.

His father went on, "For heaven's sake, Tim, why didn't you tell me?"

"I guess I was afraid to," said Tim. "I didn't know how or what to tell you, Dad, I just thought it was important to you that I play football. I didn't want to disappoint you."

Tim's Dad looked shocked. "It was important to me, Tim, because I thought you'd miss a lot of fun if you didn't play. It never occurred to me that you wouldn't like the game as much as I did." His big hand covered Tim's. "What I want for you, Tim, is for you to be happy. I thought this was a way for you to have fun. I'm sorry that you don't like sports, and that you felt you had to play—just for me."

Tim looked up, "No, no, Dad, it isn't that I don't like sports, it's that I don't like contact sports. Now, there's tennis, I love tennis!"

Mr. Anders beamed at his wife, then back at Tim and said, "Why that's great, Tim. You know, your mother was pretty good at tennis.

Maybe you got a little talent from her side of the family."

Tim's mother blushed and said, "I was not that good, Timmy, but I did enjoy the game."

Tim sought his mother's eye and said as kindly as he could, "Mom, I'm almost fourteen and I really would like it if you would call me Tim, not Timmy."

Mrs. Anders looked surprised and said, "All right Timm—I mean Tim, I'll try. Did that bird say anything about your name?"

"No," said Tim, " It's just that he made me feel a little better about myself. A little more grown up. Gratchet was a real friend. He showed me that I have to look for my own talent, and develop it, and that I have to work at what ever I choose to do to be successful."

Mr. Ander's eyebrows went up as he looked at his son and said, "My that bird certainly left an impression."

Tim turned to his mother, "I love you, Mom, I hope that you understand all this, but I really want to change my thinking. This bird happening has given me the insight to be different. Timmy is a name for a little boy. I want and need to grow up."

Mrs. Anders got up from her chair and walked around to hug her son. She put her arm around his shoulder and said, "I guess I'll have to trade my little boy for a young man. I love you too, son"

The rest of the meal was spent rather silently, each person reflecting on the change of heart in the other. After a wonderful dessert Tim looked at his parents and said, "Guess I'd better hit the books. Thanks Mom for a great supper, and thanks to both of you for understanding."

Mr. and Mrs. Anders smiled at their son, and Mr. Anders said, "Just remember we'll always be here if you need us."

Tim headed upstairs, the about halfway up he turned and said "Thanks again, you guys, for being the best parents ever."

The door to Tim's bedroom clicked shut. He walked over to the nightstand where he had put his books, and carried them to his desk across the room. He picked up his math book, opened it to the assignment, then read a couple of paragraphs. Then he re-read them. "I wish that they'd make it a little bit clearer," he thought. "Why in the heck do I need this stuff anyway? When would I ever use it"? Tim scratched his head, "Look at this, when will I ever need this junk?"

Tim suddenly looked up in surprise. "What was that?" he wondered. Then he heard the familiar flapping of wings. He turned to see Gratchet perched on the top of his desk lamp. "Oh no, not you again"?

Gratchet grinned with pleasure. "Yep, it's me ol' buddy. I must say, you were really great downstairs. Both of your parents were really proud of you. You really made them aware of what your projected desires are."

Tim looked surprised, "Proud of me?" he asked, "Do you really think so?"

"Yes, I do." He moved closer to Tim and said, "Having trouble with your math?"

"No, not really," he felt silly talking to a bird. "What good is it? I mean, when will I ever use this junk?" Tim slapped his hand across the page of his math book, and the assignment for the day.

Gratchet rolled his eyes and looked at Tim. "Tim, think of everything that you are assigned to do as stairsteps up to your real goal."

Gratchet spread out his wings and said, "You have to grow and learn little by little, not in one big gigantic swoop." Gratchet dropped down on the desk, hopped over to the other side, put one wing on his hip and said, "Think of it this way, Tim, each assignment is a stair step to your small goal. Get the idea? Each small goal completed is a large step to a higher goal." Gratchet tilted his head and winked at Tim. "Know what I mean?" he asked. "The assignments that are given are all stairs to a higher learning...that's where you gotta end up to achieve success. Right?"

Tim gave him a warm smile. Gratchet went on, "You see, if you will take note, the easiest math lessons are in the first part of the math book. The hardest are on the last pages. Now, the ones in between are very important because each one is a step in learning. You can't reach the next level unless you stand on the step beneath it, one at a time. Make it a game, Tim, and every assignment you can look at with pride as another step toward your goal." Gratchet stepped closer, "Are you having trouble with the problems?"

"No, not really," said Tim, "I was just questioning why they are important and now, thanks to you, I know why." Tim turned to his books and was soon deep into his homework. He didn't even notice when Gratchet hopped back on the lamp, jumped in the air, and sailed silently out the window.

Tim charged through his math assignments. He made notes where he was not totally sure of the answer. He'd check with his teacher the next day.

The rest of Tim's studies went very well, and after he finished he sat back and smiled "There's a lot to be said for Gratchet's stairstep idea," he thought. "My homework never went so fast. I've learned too, that life is a series of stairsteps. I guess that's where the expression, 'one step at a time' comes from."

Tim's whole outlook on life and his future had changed. From now on everything was going to be great. Not necessarily easy, but obtainable, one day at a time.

STOOPLE

Are there things on your mind that are taking up room,
So the thoughts that you weave all get snagged in the loom?

Stoople forgets and will help you discard
The thoughts to leave out when the thinking is hard.

The brain can get stuffed with useless illusion,
You need to forget to contend with confusion.

Don't allow pieces of thoughts you don't need,
To grow in your mind like a festering weed.

He'll spray out your mind and then let it sow
The seeds for ideas that you want to grow.

Let Stoople forget what is bothering you,
Just say "forget it" and that he will do.

PETER AND STOOPLE

All the sad events of the past two years passed through Peter's mind as he sat in the station waiting for the call to board the train to the west. The Mother Superior stood like a pillar, waiting too for the train to take away the young boy she had taken care of for two years.

The small farm where Peter grew up was a beautiful place. It was tucked in a valley that was always lush with green, and in the spring flowers were everywhere. Peter smiled as he recalled the giggles of his little sisters as they gathered the flowers, all with stems too short.

There was always enough food, warm clothes, and in the winter a warm and cozy house to call home. Peter's recollection of his mother was of discipline, lots of love, hearty and tasty cooking, hugs and encouragement to do the very best he could. His father was Peter's mentor. They did everything together, hunting, fishing, farming, and all the repairs around the farm. Peter and his father had also spent a lot of time gardening, and it was one of his favorite memories. His father was strong, strict, but kind and patient at the same time. In order to teach Peter he would go over something as many times as it took for Peter to learn it. The tears rolled down Peter's face as he thought of them all, and home, everything gone forever. "I can never go home," he thought to himself.

Peter was at school when it happened. No one had realized that the war was so close. Then the shelling began. Later it was reported that the bombing and shelling of the farm was a mistake, "A lot of good it does to know that," thought Peter bitterly.

The cottage had been hit first, and Peter's mother and sisters were killed instantly. His father had been in the barn, and upon hearing the noise ran for the house. The shelling that followed killed him, too. Peter was left with no one. His home, his family, his security were all swept away in just a few moments.

Then the memories of the Orphanage came into focus. Peter was miserable there. The nuns tried their best, but their capabilities and funds were limited. Nothing nor no one could mend Peter's broken heart or bring back the family he loved so much.

Peter was nine years old when he was sent to the Orphanage. He was overcome with grief and disappointment, and had become some- what withdrawn. No one had much sympathy to give, as most of the children had been through much the same thing as Peter had.

Two very bleak and sad years followed. Peter was a good boy, and his obedience was appreciated when there were so many to take care of. He was surprised when the message came for him to report to the Mother Superior. "What did I do wrong?" he had wondered to himself.

Peter pushed open the huge oak door to the Mother Superior's of- fice. When he timidly peeked in, she waved him in without looking up and without a trace of a smile. She indicated with a nod of her head that he was to sit down. "This one is special," the Mother thought to herself. "He's bright, innovative, and so good—but wait, don't let your emotions get involved, you know you're always heartbroken when they leave." Then she looked up at Peter and said, "Peter, you'll be leaving us."

Peter was shocked. "Why Mother? What have I done? Where would I go?" Peter felt a sudden rush of panic.

"You are going to America to live with your Uncle Stephan. He is your father's younger brother. He and his wife have no children and have sent the money and the request that you go with them," said Mother Superior. She kept her head down and fussed with the papers on her desk so that Peter would not see her tears.

"Where do they live?" asked Peter.

"They live in Springfield Ohio in the U.S.A. Good thing you have learned your English so well," said the Mother Superior.

"Yes, good thing," answered Peter. "What a fine surprise, I wonder what it will be like?" Peter thought to himself.

He had been instructed to pack his few belongings, say his good-byes, and be ready to leave in the morning early.

Peter left the Mother Superior's office and went down the long hall to the back door of the building. He paused a moment at the top of the stairs outside, then he went right to vegetable garden out back. The garden had been Peter's special project since he had been at the Orphanage, as it always reminded him of his father and home. Peter said to no one in particular, "Well, I guess this garden will just have to grow on without me."

Peter was suddenly overwhelmed with homesickness, loneliness, and heartbreak. He knelt down beside the garden and wept bitterly.

"That's enough crying, Peter," said a voice. Peter looked all around and saw no one.

"You must forget what has happened to you and prepare yourself to get on with your life. You must begin to allow yourself to be happy," said the voice.

Then, to Peter's amazement, a small figure came from behind the little shoots of corn. The figure seemed to stretch and stretch until he was about the size of a small boy.

"What in the world?" said Peter. "Just who are you anyway, and where did you come from?"

"I'm Stoople," said the figure. "I have come from the Island of Corkle to help you forget the past, and look forward to your future. You have a whole new world opening up for you. You are going to have to let go and end the despair and unhappiness you are feeling."

"I don't know if I can do that," said Peter. " All I can think of is how much I loved them all."

"I'm sure you loved your family, Peter, this is the reason you must let go. To go to America was your father's dream. Now you have a chance to live that dream for him."

"How can I let them go, I love them all so much." said Peter, his eyes were again filling with tears.

"Grow up, Peter," said Stoople. "You have to decide to just let go, you are almost a man, now grow up and be happy. Now that you are going to America you have every opportunity to do just that. I have to be on my way now. Remember, just do it!" said Stoople as he shrank to a very small size and magically vanished behind the radishes.

Peter thought to himself, "Was he real or did I imagine him?" Peter knew that what Stoople was saying was right, but he was doubtful that he could forget. It was as though the memories were all he had left.

Peter struggled to his feet and wiped the tears from his face on his sleeve, then looked longingly once more at the garden. He picked himself up and walked slowly up the steps into the Orphanage. He had to pack and say his goodbyes.

The Mother Superior took Peter in the wiggly old cart to the Rail Station the next morning. Peter's uncle in America had sent money for the rail trip to Frankfurt, and the air trip from there to Ohio in America. It was all so new, so exciting, so scary, a boy of eleven traveling to the U.S.A all alone. "Many have done it before," thought Peter, "I will be all right."

Peter sat there in the station with the I.D. and the travel instructions hung around his neck. "I feel like a goose headed for the market," he thought to himself.

The voice on the speaker was hard to understand, but Peter finally heard his train being announced. He had butterflies in his stomach as the Mother Superior straightened his collar. She led him to the steps of the train, and let go finally to watch him get on the train. She stood in the station like a sentinel to watch until the train was out of sight. Then she turned slowly, wiped the tears away and blew her nose before she climbed back into the cart and made her way home to the Orphanage.

The train trip was uneventful. Peter was content to watch as the spring countryside swept by him. "I wonder if I'll ever see the valley again now that I go to America." he thought quietly.

When Peter arrived at the train station in Frankfurt, there was a lady from the airlines there waiting for him. As he stepped from the train he felt very important as he saw his name on a waving cardboard sign in the train station. The lady moved the sign excitedly so that Peter would see her.

Peter had been instructed to go with the lady to the airport. She was very friendly, and made an attempt to be sociable, but Peter was not too interested in her talk. He was thinking about the airplane, the long trip, and frankly he was scared to death! The lady escorted Peter to the boarding gate. He had only one small bag, so he didn't have to check luggage through the baggage area.

When it was time to board the big 747 Peter's heart was thumping madly. He turned to the lady who had assisted him and said, with a slight forced smile, "Thank you for all your kindness. I wish you health and good fortune always." The speech he had learned the night before, and he was happy for no mistakes. With that he turned and walked down the covered entryway onto the plane.

Peter settled himself in his seat. He looked around and noticed that the other passengers were fastening their seatbelts and stowing their carry-on luggage under their seats. A very kind lady in the uniform of the airlines smiled and whispered that she would be back later to tell Peter all about what to expect.

Suddenly the huge aircraft jerked and then slowly backed out and away from the terminal. It turned and started out toward the runway and take-off point. Peter was nearly wild with excitement.

There was quiet inside the big airliner as the pilot made ready to take off. Peter was watching as much as he could through the porthole on his side. All of a sudden, they were racing down the runway, faster, and faster, until all at once the airplane left the ground and with ease headed skyward. Peter watched as the buildings below became smaller and the plane surged forward and up into the clouds.

A few minutes later there was the sound of some soft bells, and right after that the stewardess who had talked to Peter before came and sat down beside him.

"Peter Petrovich," she said and Peter nodded, "I will be with you for the whole trip, even on to Cincinnati."

"Cincinnati?" said Peter, "I thought we are going to New York."

"We are going to New York," said the stewardess, then we have to catch another flight to Cincinnati where your uncle and aunt will meet us. There you will drive with your aunt and uncle to your new home in Springfield, Ohio."

Peter smiled and said, "Good! Now how long before we get to New York?"

The stewardess answered, "Just a little over 12 hours. Then there will be another flight from New York to Cincinnati, which will take about two and a half hours. So you could put the flight time at around fourteen hours, plus the terminal time in New York when we change planes."

"Good!" answered Peter, then he said, "Are you sure they have enough petrol for all that time and distance?"

The stewardess smiled and said, "Don't worry about a thing Peter, everything is ready to go. Here, read the menu, then why not think about what you would like to eat? Let the pilot and the crew be concerned about the flight. They really do know what they are doing."

"Oh my," thought Peter, "all this, the train, the plane and now food too, it must have cost my uncle a great deal of money..maybe he's rich,"

After a little while the comfortable warmth of the cabin, plus the steady hum of the engines, had Peter rubbing his eyes. It had been very early when he got out of bed this morning, and now he felt the exhaustion that excitement generates. Peter fell fast asleep. He dreamed about the family, and the valley, and the farm. They were all there, their laughing faces all around him.

When Peter awakened he was surprised to find out where he was. He suddenly realized that every mile was taking him farther and farther away from home. All at once he was terribly homesick and he longed for his family with all his heart. He so wished they could have shared this wonderful adventure with him. Tears filled his eyes again, and he said to himself, "Someday, when I make my fortune I will come back and visit it all."

Peter was astounded at the ease with which the pilot landed the big 747. Most of the scenery had been just a sea of clouds, and Peter was glad to be on the ground again.

The people on the airplane began to stir from their naps as they taxied into the terminal. The stewardess came up to Peter and said, "Stay here Peter until I come for you. We need to get all these people de-planed and on their way." She hurried to the front of the plane, but was back shortly. "This is it, Peter Petrovich, this is where we get off."

Peter and the stewardess hurried through the terminal. Peter looked about in wonder. "It's so big, and it's so grand," he thought to himself.

They stopped briefly at customs, and then followed the signs to the gate that was on their ticket.

All of a sudden he looked up at the sign- "Gate 68." The stewardess took his hand and they both went through the gate and on to a smaller plane.

The journey to Cincinnati was uneventful. Peter was curious about what to expect. "Will they like me?" he thought. "Will I be welcome?" Then when they landed in Cincinnati and left the plane his fears disappeared. There in the crowd waiting for the arriving plane was a man and a woman holding a cardboard sign which read, "Welcome to the USA Peter Petrovich."

Peter stood still for a moment. He was struck with the resemblance of his Uncle Stephan to his father. His aunt was very pretty, and had kind laughing eyes like his mother.

After what seemed like hours, Peter broke into a huge smile and ran toward the couple. Suddenly they were running toward Peter too, all were laughing and crying and hugging at the same time. It was good to feel the loving hugs of this aunt and uncle. "This feels almost like home," thought Peter.

The stewardess had Peter's uncle sign some papers and with a smile for everyone she said, "Well Mr. Petrovich, he's all yours," then she turned to Peter and said, " Welcome to the USA Peter, be happy." Then she was gone.

Peter, his aunt and his uncle went out of the terminal and headed toward the parking area. "How will you ever find your automobile, Uncle with all the other cars here? " asked Peter.

Uncle Stephan smiled, "No problem, Peter, you get used to it all in time. By the way, this is your Aunt Beth." Peter nodded approvingly

The expressway amazed Peter, so many cars going so fast darting in and out. "How do they remember it all, where they are going and where they have been?" Peter asked smiling.

"Like your uncle said, Peter, you'll get used to it" laughed Aunt Beth.

They pulled up in front of a modest brick home on a neat and shady street in Springfield. Peter was all eyes, it was beautiful, not like anything in the village back home, but beautiful.

They went up the steps to the front door. Uncle Stephan unlocked the door and stepped aside, "You first, Peter, Welcome home."

Peter entered, then turned and looked at both his aunt and uncle. The tears came, and he hugged then both. "Thank you, Uncle, thank you, thank you." It was an emotional homecoming to be sure!

Aunt Beth called, "Peter, come see your room, it's all ready for you."

Peter went down the hall, amazed that he was to have a room all his own. He looked into the room which was to be his. He couldn't believe his eyes. There was a desk and chair for study, a wonderful big bed with a bright coverlet that Aunt Beth had made herself. There was a bookcase, with many books. "A dictionary!" said Peter, "am I to have my own dictionary to use?" Peter was overjoyed.

"Everything in this room is your own, Peter," said Aunt Beth.

Peter put down his satchel, walked around the room looking at it all, touching, exploring everything, and then he stopped and tried the bed. He bounced a little, then looked up at his smiling aunt and uncle and said, "It's a nice room," not knowing just what to say about their generosity.

They all ended up in the kitchen catching up on what happened to Peter's family, and how Uncle Stephan had come to America. Aunt Beth made some tea, and she had made a wonderful cake for them to eat. They talked until late, the excitement and emotion wouldn't have let them sleep anyway.

The next few weeks were busy with schedule arrangements for school. Peter also needed to find out all about his surroundings. He had to learn that American slang was different from traditional English . Everything was different from his home on the farm and the orphanage. It took time to get used to it all, so that he could get around on his own and become a real member of his new family.

After a couple of months, Uncle Stephan noticed that Peter was adjusting well, but he was not happy. "I wonder what we could do to help him overcome the terrible things that have happened to him," he thought to himself.

It was at breakfast a couple of days later that Uncle Stephan asked Peter, "If there was one thing we could do for you that would really make you happy, what would that be Peter?"

Peter smiled at him and surprised them both by saying, "I would love to plant a garden. There's some unused ground in the back yard that would be perfect for a garden. Would it be possible to start right away?"

"Done!" said Uncle Stephan. "Would you mind if I help you, Peter?"

"I would love that" said Peter with a grin. The garden became the big project. Peter enjoyed it because he spent time with Uncle Stephan, and it was almost like being with his father. The garden flourished and soon the tender shoots became plants that promised to be delicious meals. Peter would spend a lot of time sitting out by the garden looking over each crop—remembering. "Why? why?" he'd ask himself over and over. I love Uncle Stephan and Aunt Beth, but why did I have to lose my whole family. I remember....... then one day Peter's thoughts were interrupted by a voice.

"That's the trouble with you, Peter, you remember too much." Peter looked around and at first he saw no one. Then out from under a lettuce leaf came the gnome-like creature. He was small at first, but then as before, right in front of Peter's eyes, he stretched up again to become the size of a small boy.

Peter stared at him for a few minutes then asked, "Not you again! "Who are you, again, and how do you do that?"

"I'm Stoople, the stretching is just my way of getting your attention. " He put his thumbs into the straps of his overalls and said to Peter."

"Your mind can be stuffed with useless illusion, you need to forget to contend with confusion.

"What do you mean?" asked Peter.

"You have been remembering over and over all the things that happened to you in Europe. You can do nothing now to change things. You can only look ahead. You need to forget," said Stoople.

"Forget my family? " Never!" exclaimed Peter.

"You misunderstand me," said Stoople." I mean you need to take the memories out of your head, and put them into your heart for safe keeping. This will give room for the building of the life that is before you. Peter, when we mourn too long, or keep resentment and anger in our minds, it keeps us from thinking constructively."

"What do you mean?" asked Peter.

"I mean that bitterness comes from anger and sorrow that has been on your mind for a long time. You cannot be happy if you're bitter. Pretty soon your mind is thinking of little else and you are not only unhappy yourself, but you make everyone around you unhappy as well," said Stoople.

"How do I begin?" asked Peter.

"Maybe it would be a good idea to begin right where you are. Grab and hold on tight to the happiness that your aunt and uncle are trying so hard to give you. They want so much to be loving adoptive parents. Show them that you are grateful for the home they have given you. Make them proud, as proud as your parents would have been, by being the best you can be, in your conduct, your school and in your attitude about life." said Stoople.

Peter studied the little character for a few moments and then said, "You are right, of course. I have everything any boy could want or need and I'm so full of self-pity I can't see the good that is all around me. Thank you, Stoople. I'm really going to do better, but what do I do about the things I can't forget?"

"You give them to me," said Stoople. "and I will spray out your mind and then let it sow the seeds for ideas that you want to grow."

With that Stoople shrank down to a very small size, and disappeared under the beets. Peter looked and looked but could not find Stoople anywhere.

"What are you looking for?" The voice of Uncle Stephan right behind him startled Peter.

Peter smiled and answered "I guess you might say I'm looking for myself."

"I don't understand, Peter," said his uncle.

"Neither do I Uncle Stephen, but in time I will, yes, in time I will."

Peter stood, reached up and put his arms around his uncle and held him tight.

BLAMMITT

A temper that's lost can be so hard to find,
A top that is blown can be hard on the mind.

No need for your blood to be pressured this way,
No need for a tantrum to ruin your day.

Let Blammitt take over your anger for you,
To keep you from doing the harm you might do.

He'll check with his gauge to see just how mad,
He's got to get before you get bad,

He'll throw things and scream and use words profane,
You're cool as an ice cube and fresh as the rain.

He's stamping his feet and seeing bright red,
Your calm is collected, for he's mad instead.

TOM AND BLAMMITT

Tom Polenski lived, breathed and existed for the fun of playing baseball. He had an outstanding pitching arm, batted .375 consistently, and was an excellent fielder in any position. His favorite position, however, was first base. The reason he was still in the minor leagues was that he had a temper that was explosive, unreasonable, and once aroused, completely out of hand.

Tom was "Movie Star" handsome. The girls always made a big fuss over him until they witnessed one of his temper tantrums. That usually turned them off like a switch.

Tom was not really aware of the reaction to his temper. Growing up in a home where you yelled and screamed and fought openly to achieve your way or get your goal accomplished, he thought he was pretty normal. He assumed that temper and "macho" were one and the same. "A good fight only makes the situation more interesting," was his way of thinking. So it was that whenever he became frustrated or upset, he let the temper fly. It solved nothing, and in the end brought him nothing but trouble.

Being in the minor leagues Tom traveled quite a bit. He had no roots, so he really didn't mind being away, he didn't even have a steady girl. Besides, Melissa Campbell was really the only girl that mattered to Tom. "That's over with," he thought to himself sadly as he recalled the events that brought about their breakup.

Melissa and Tom had been getting on quite well. More and more they were thought of as a twosome, and everyone expected that it was serious. Tom had met Melissa when the team was playing a scheduled game at home.

Tom was playing first base that afternoon. The lead batter stepped up to the plate. Tom heard the crack of the bat and saw a foul ball that was hit high and to his left. Tom looked skyward and fielded the ball on a dead run. Just as he made the catch he went crashing into the bleachers. When he caught the ball the crowd cheered wildly, and Tom looked up with a smile to face the stands. When he gazed up into the crowd all he could see was Melissa. She took his breath away, she was so beautiful. Her lovely blond hair cascaded down past her shoulders, and the way the afternoon sun hit the blonde halo that surrounded Melissa's face made her look like an angel. She was wearing a light pink sun dress that showed off her tan skin. Tom stared for a moment "I have to meet that girl," he thought to himself.

Tom wasted no time. When he got back to the dugout he asked one of his team mates, Ted Polsun, "Who is that girl? You know, the blond?"

"Oh, that's the new city manager's daughter. She's a knockout all right, I guess just about everyone would love to get to know her. She's quite a lady too. Her name is Melissa, Melissa Campbell."

"Can you give me an introduction?" asked Tom.

"I'll see what I can do, but no promises," answered Ted. But somehow Ted did come through with an introduction, and Tom managed the courage to ask Melissa for a date.

Tom's first date with Melissa was wonderful. He found out that she had just moved to Brockton from the East. They went out for a bite to eat, and spent the rest of the evening getting acquainted with each other. They talked until late, and Tom found that he had shared things with Melissa that he had never shared with anyone before. Things like where he hoped to go with his baseball career, and what long term plans he had for his future.

When Tom took Melissa home he told her it was the greatest evening of his whole life. Melissa agreed. There was really no doubt about it, Tom and Melissa were going to be seeing a lot of each other..

There was a round of wonderful times when Tom and the team stayed in Brockton. The team traveled for half their games so as a result Tom and Melissa didn't see each other as much as they would have liked.

Then it happened. During an important home game Tom was playing first base. It was the last of the ninth, his team was leading 3-2 and there were two outs, but the visiting team had the bases loaded and their most powerful hitter came up to bat. He hit a ground ball to Tom's right that should have been an easy out, but Tom fumbled it. Then having missed the play at first base, he threw the ball over the catcher's head in an attempt to keep the winning run from reaching home.

Tom left the field feeling disgraced. He went to the dugout, sat down, and put his head in his hands. He felt awful. He felt he had lost the game all by himself. After a few of his team mates patted his back, saying, "Come on Tom, we'll get them next time," Tom finally realized that all players have their moments of defeat. The sad thing was that Tom's errors that night did cost the team the game.

Melissa was waiting for him after the game. "What a mess I made of the game tonight," Tom said to Melissa as they made their way toward the parking area. Tom was really upset about the loss.

"No one is perfect all the time," said Melissa. "This was only tonight, and you've played so well all year I wouldn't give it a second thought. Come on Tom, lets forget it, and better luck next time, O.K.?"

Melissa smiled up at him and Tom couldn't help but smile back at her, "O.K.," he said. Somehow Melissa seemed to make everything all right with just her smile.

They went to Antonio's, a favorite dinner house. It was a quiet establishment where local celebrities gathered for a light supper. Tom and Melissa had forgotten the game and the loss, and were deep in conversation when Tom heard his name being called out.

"Hey, Polenski, you big stupid clumsy jerk, how did you get on the Brockton team anyhow? You sure loused up the night for me, I lost ten dollars on that game tonight. They sure scraped the bottom of the bowl when they signed you."

All eyes turned toward a man staggering out of the bar, as he advanced toward Tom and Melissa, Tom's face turned red with fury. He slowly pushed his chair away from the table and stood up. He was facing a man who clearly was trouble looking for a place to happen, and happen it did to the dismay of Melissa. She looked upon the whole scene with horror, disbelief and embarrassment.

"Just who are you calling stupid and clumsy," roared Tom, pushing the man's chest with his fingertips. Tom's face was twisted with rage.

'You, fumble fingers" said the man. "Maybe we should take up a little collection and get you a seeing eye dog."

"Come on, Tom," said Melissa. "Lets go, he's had too much to drink. Don't lower yourself, he's just looking for attention. Please, Tom, lets go."

"Stay out of this, Melissa." Tom gave her an angry look.

Melissa was taken back. "Tom, come on, fighting solves nothing." Melissa had never seen Tom like this.

Tom turned on her, and said with a slow deliberate voice, "Melissa, I said stay out of this." Then he added a few swear words, and his expression was one Melissa had not seen before. Her eyes widened and then filled with tears. She put on her coat, gathered her purse and gloves and left. She called a taxi and was gone.

"Looks like your girl can't stand the sight of you either," taunted the man, "and looks like she's too good for you anyway."

Tom was out of control. He grabbed the trouble maker by the front of his shirt and shoved him backwards over a table. When the man came staggering to his feet he lunged at Tom and soon the two of them were rolling around crashing into things. The fight had developed into a real brawl.

When it was over Tom was nursing a bleeding nose, a terrible bruise on his shoulder, and a black eye. The guy who had started it all was fighting for consciousness, as his friends tried to arouse him enough to get him up and out of the restaurant.

Tom looked around for Melissa, and suddenly when he realized that she had left without him his heart sank. Dragging himself up he staggered out the door into the night, all the while holding his bloody nose. When he got home he called Melissa.

"What kind of a girl are you anyway Melissa, cutting out on a guy in the middle of a fight?"

"You know I hate fighting Tom," said Melissa "It never solves anything, and many times it just makes things worse. I wasn't about to stand by and watch you make a fool of yourself. My father would not like to hear that I was with a brawling escort."

"Would you have me let that guy get away with what he said to me?" yelled Tom.

"What does it matter what he said to you? It doesn't make it true. Oh Tom, when will you let go of the anger and clean up your language? When you do some soul searching to make some changes, we'll talk," said Melissa.

"Listen, lady," shouted Tom, "this is the way I am. You may as well know that now. I don't take any insults from anybody. You got that? Not even you. You can take it or leave it, Melissa."

"I want nothing to do with bad taste, temper tantrums, and violence, so I guess I'll leave it," said Melissa." Good night, Tom." She gently hung the phone back in its cradle.

That was the last time Tom talked to or heard from Melissa Campbell.

The phone did ring a little later, but it was only the manager of Antonio's letting him know that a bill for damages would be forthcoming.

Tom laid his sore body back on the bed and folded his arms in back of his head. He lay there staring at the ceiling. He sure was going to miss Melissa. He wondered if the fight was worth it. The tears started in his eyes and rolled down his cheeks. Depression was about to take over when all of a sudden Tom heard a voice say, "Boy, you sure do have a knack for making a mess of things."

Tom was startled, "What are you supposed to be? " He sat up and stared at an ugly creature sitting on a chair near his bed.

"I'm not supposed to be, — I AM Blammitt," said the creature.

"Who? Come on, what do you take me for. I know you're just some sort of illusion," said Tom. "Either that or I've lost it completely."

With that Blammitt reached over and pinched Tom's arm as hard as he could. Tom yelled out loud.

"What the h—- are you doing? That hurt." He shook his fist at Blammitt. He was about to swing, but the little creature blocked his arm.

"Yes, I suppose it did hurt, but now I have your attention and you know you're not dreaming." Blammitt uttered a couple of tsk tsk's, "Look at you. All bruised up. And the way you treated Melissa, you were terrible. You really hurt her you know. She was not only hurt but she was humiliated in front of everyone in Antonio's."

"What's that to you? This whole thing is really none of your business or anyone else's you know," said Tom defensively.

"You are going to mess up your life, Tom, if you don't stop these temper outbursts. I overheard your coach Evans say that they want to give you a chance to talk to one of the major league coaches, but with your temper, they feel that you're still too immature," said Blammitt. "Tell me, just what is it that makes you so angry anyway?"

"I don't know," said Tom, suddenly sad. "When something happens and I get mad, I just lose it. It's inside me. I can't seem to help myself." Tom leaned back and looked down at his hands. "You know I really powdered that guy, look at the bruises on my hands. They already feel stiff and sore." Tom rubbed his hands, "This is not going to help my batting or my throwing."

"It doesn't help your heart either," said Blammitt. "A nasty temper is what they call type 'A' behavior. It makes your blood pressure go up. That's definitely not good for the heart, and besides, Tom, you don't feel good about yourself or get any satisfaction after it's all over do you?"

"Not really," said Tom sadly, "and now I've lost Melissa, the best thing that has ever happened to me. I don't know why I do these things. What makes me blow up? What's the matter with me anyway? How can I change? Why can't I just let it roll off my back like some of the other guys?"

"It all has to do with attitude, Tom. You go looking for a fight, and you'll always find one, Why not go looking for the good in people?" said Blammitt. "When you got into that fight tonight, that was silly, you could have looked at that bloke and said, "Guess I was clumsy, we all have our off nights." Then you could have let it go at that. If he got out of hand, you could have left like Melissa wanted you to. You didn't have to prove anything. I think that the guy was looking for a notch on his belt."

"What do you mean?" asked Tom.

"I mean that he was hoping to be able to brag that he beat you up to make him look important. What made you react the way you did anyway?"

"When he said what he did I just saw red," said Tim. "There are times that I don't like myself either, and when someone says something to put me down, I just blow up."

"I know that," said Blammitt. "And that's what I'm going to do for you."

"What?" said Tom. "You're going to do what for me?"

"I'm going to be angry, get mad, lose it, see red, throw things, swear, all that, " said Blammitt, "so that you can remain calm, cool, and collected. You are going to tuck me into the back of your mind, so that when you start to lose your temper I'm going to smack you with a mallet on the back of your brains. When you learn to keep cool emotionally, and stay in control I won't bother you anymore. We're going to break you of this temper thing if you'll let us. How about it Tom, will you give it a try?"

"Sure, I can try," said Tom, "what have I got to lose?" Tom could hardly believe that this whole scene was happening, He really felt that it was all a fantasy and that he would laugh about it in the morning.

Then Blammitt said, "One thing that you need to learn, Tom, is that you are special. Not only with your baseball talent, but the person you are. There is only one Tom Polenski, and your responsibility should be to make him the best there is."

The following day the team was up early. Tom had pretty well settled it in his head that the whole encounter with Blammitt was a dream or an illusion of some kind. He thought a lot about it on the bus ride. Blammitt was right though, Tom needed to improve his attitude, and he needed to keep his emotions in check. The whole day was one of rest and relaxation, quiet and reflection for Tom. When his team mates asked him to go out with them Tom declined. "I'm going to turn in early." he said and then he smiled, "Besides, I need to stay out of trouble."

The guys smiled and let him go. They liked Tom even though they knew he had some changing to do. They all felt that Tom really had big league potential. They were sorry to hear of his break up with Melissa, she seemed so good for him.

Tom checked into his room at the hotel. The team was staying over. He took off his jacket and hung it up. Then he shed his shoes and tie and just lay back and relaxed against the pillows on his bed. He was remembering the last few days, going over them in his head. Suddenly, there was Blammitt again, at the foot of the bed, gazing at him intently.

"Not you again, Blammitt." said Tom. "I was just thinking about you."

"Yep, it's me again." said Blammitt. "I need to give you some pearls of wisdom to think about."

"Like what?" said Tom.

"Well," said Blammitt," If you're so quick to accept an insult from a drunken stranger as the truth, I have to believe that you must not like yourself very much."

"What's that supposed to mean?" said Tom.

"It means that if you don't like yourself, you're going to have a terrible time really liking anyone else. An ugly comment would only confirm what you already think about yourself. You have been given the idea that you have to fight your way out of things. Somewhere along the line as you have grown up, you have been told that you are not a good person, and that you're a 'know nothing' individual. This is not the case, Tom. Your potential to be a great baseball star or whatever else you choose to be is unlimited, and the opportunity to realize your dreams is knocking your door down," said Blammitt.

"So? How do I change things? said Tom.

"You can start by making a list of the good things you know you have, including talent. Then make another list of the failures you have had. I think that you will find that the good things far outweigh the bad," said Blammitt. "I think you will find too, that the failures were really learning experiences that we all have to go through to grow up."

"You're helping me to sort things out," said Tom. "Maybe I'll be able to get it together and put the anger behind me, with your help. I really appreciate this, Blammitt."

"You'll be surprised, Tom, how well it works," said Blammitt. "Go ahead, feel good about who you are and what your talents are. We are all someone special and when we know this about ourselves, it just makes life a little easier, and it helps us to appreciate others."

The next day the team left for the field early so they could loosen up and get in a little batting practice. Tom was in a very good frame of mind and was hoping that coach Evans would ask him to pitch. Tom took it very well when the coach asked him to take second base. "We really need you there, Tom," said coach Evans "And I want you to bat cleanup."

Tom wasn't too thrilled about second base, but when he started to say something about it, there was a light tap on the back of his head. Instead he said. "OK, Coach, I'll be glad to do what I can."

Tom took his place at second base as the game got started. His energy was high, his reflexes were cat-like, and his spirits were soaring. He played an outstanding first five innings. Then in the sixth inning, the pitcher of the opposite team was up to bat. He hit a line drive out the first base line. The first baseman picked up the ball, and then when he went to step to first base for the base tag, he dropped the ball. The runner advanced then on to second. The first baseman picked up the ball and threw it to second. Tom quickly scooped up the ball, and when he went to touch second, the runner came into the base with cleats up. Tom made the out, but the runner's cleats gouged him badly. Tom pulled himself to his feet and looked down at the man at his feet. He felt his face turn red, and was about to start raging when he felt a smack at the back of his head. "Blammitt," he thought to himself. Then instead of anger, he felt compassion. He reached down to pull the man to his feet.

"Are you OK, Buddy?" asked Tom.

"Yeah, how about you? Gee I'm sure sorry, that's a bad gash on your leg," said the other team's pitcher.

Tom's Coach Evans called for a time out. As Tom limped off the field everyone stood and cheered him. "Wow, this is a good feeling," said Tom to himself as he looked up at the cheering fans.

Tom was going to be out of the line-up for a few days due to his leg injury. Back in his room as he read his hometown's newspaper account of the game, Tom was a little embarrassed that the paper would make such a big deal of his kindness toward the base runner who gashed his leg. "All I did was help him to his feet, this is silly," said Tom to himself.

"Yes, but a week ago you would have decked him." It was Blammitt perched on the chest of drawers. "You would have started a brawl right there on the baseball diamond. You know that's true. You see Tom, fans like to see their heroes act like gentlemen."

"Oh, hi, Blammitt. I guess I have to admit it felt pretty nice to be cheered instead of jeered." Tom grinned at his funny little buddy.

Then Blammitt said, "You see, Tom, you must learn that if another person approaches you with anger, he is a fool. If you react with anger, then you're a bigger fool than he is." Blammitt then disappeared and Tom was smiling as he turned the lights out and went to sleep.

Tom healed fast, and played the rest of the schedule with outstanding results. There were times when his temper would start to flare, but Blammitt would whack him one, and Tom little by little learned to deal with life without anger. Tom was much more relaxed, and was beginning to like his new attitude. The fans loved it, he was making a vast number of new friends and they made him their special hero. Blammitt visited him from time to time just to keep Tom on his toes.

The team finally came home to Brockton where they were greeted by the fans as they got off the bus. They had a fabulous road trip, winning all but one of their games It looked very much as if they would take the league pennant with no trouble at all.

Tom left the bus and headed for his car. Then he drove on home looking forward to a good night's sleep in his own bed.

He had been home only a few minutes when the phone rang. It was Coach Evans.

"Polenski, I want to see you in my office tomorrow before batting practice. There are a few things that I would like to go over with you.

"Yes Sir," answered Tom, with a million questions in his mind. "I'll be there."

"See you then, goodbye," said Coach Evans.

"Wonder what that's all about." The voice startled him and Tom whirled around to see Blammitt again perched on the chest of drawers.

"Blammitt you nearly scared the— the —ah stuffing out of me, " said Tom.

"Well, what do you think Coach Evans wants?" asked Blammitt.

"I can't imagine," said Tom. "I know I haven't done anything wrong. My batting has been the best ever." Tom frowned, "Darned if I know. I'll have to wait until tomorrow to find out. Now, Blammitt, if you don't mind I'm beat, and I'd like to get some sleep. So if you'll excuse me."

"Yeah, sure," said Blammitt. "I doubt if you'll be needing me much anymore anyway. See you later, Tom, good luck buddy."

"Thanks," said Tom, and Blammitt was gone.

The next morning Tom was outside Coach Evan's office a half hour before batting practice. The door to the coach's office finally opened and Coach Evans smiled at Tom, and gestured toward a chair.

"Sit down, Tom," he said.

"Thank you sir," said Tom, easing himself into the chair the coach had indicated.

"I'll get right to the point, "said Coach Evans. "I think that you know that we have been watching you for some time with the idea of sending you up to the majors for a try out. You have done so well the last part of this season, and your attitude is so much better, we have decided to give you a try at showing all of them what you can do. How would you feel about that?"

"Why, that's great, to have the chance to play in the major league, sir, that's my dream. Yes sir, I would like that very much." Tom was almost breathless with surprise and excitement.

"The season is almost over, Tom," said Coach Evans, "When we end the play-offs you'll need to start making your plans to leave. If I can help you Tom, just let me know. By the way, be sure and check your mail box on the way out, you've got some mail.

"Thank you, sir, for everything." Tom called over his shoulder as he opened the door to go.

Back home in his apartment kitchenette Tom laid the mail on the table and went over to make a cup of cocoa. He took the cocoa and the mail to his favorite chair and sat down. He went through the pieces of mail one by one sorting ads from the other mail—then he saw the envelope. It was from Melissa! He tore it open excitedly and read:

"Dear Tom:

I'm so proud of the changes you have made. I've been reading all about you in the newspaper. I'm happy that you have won so many games. You ought to take the season. I'd love to see you.

Love, Melissa."

Tom threw the letter up in the air with a loud YAHOO. He picked up the phone and tried the Campbell number. No answer.

The next day there was no opportunity to get in touch with Melissa. He tried several times, and either the line was busy or there was no answer. Tom left a message on the answer machine.

It was Thursday night. Tom walked out onto the field with the rest of the team. As he walked along the first base line he looked up into the stands. His heart stopped. There was Melissa looking just as beautiful as the first time he saw her. She held up a sign. "Welcome home Tom, see you later?" Tom nodded and waved in agreement.

When the last out was made, Tom thought to himself. "This is the end of the season in Brockton, I can look forward to baseball and a major league career. From now on I can hold my temper in check and keep my attitude acceptable, thanks to Blammitt's help. And tomorrow? Tomorrow is the first day of the rest of my life. I sure am one happy, lucky guy." He looked up and smiled at the beaming Melissa.

ILLCH

Illch is unhealthy, he always feels ill,
And boasts of an ailment for every known pill.

If every symptom just fits your description
Illch is the one who will fill your prescription.

Whatever the illness, he's happy to say,
He's had them all and is wasting away.

To be sick is his job so you can feel great.
He doesn't mind, so why should you wait?

Get out of your bed and let him get in,
Steady your legs and hold up your chin.

Don't let your sickness take all of your wealth,
Good Illch will be sick, for he's bored of health.

AUNT MYRTLE AND ILLCH

Mary hung up the telephone and sighed deeply. It was Aunt Myrtle, and she was feeling ill again. Mary loved her Aunt Myrtle very much and was greatly concerned that she always seemed to suffer with something. Illness had hung over the poor lady like a vulture for years, and she seemed to expect it. "I'm going to get the flu for sure," Aunt Myrtle would say to Mary, and the flu always seemed to oblige. No matter what illness was going around Aunt Myrtle was always convinced that she was destined to get it. She usually did. It seemed to Mary that as soon as one illness disappeared, another always came along to take its place.

Aunt Myrtle's medicine cabinet held a strange fascination for Mary. She wondered how in the world pill manufacturers could think of so many sizes shapes and colors. Each bottle was labeled with a mysterious title, which could have come from Latin or Greek, making the items seem much more mysterious than the simple formula they were.

Aunt Myrtle had all the sickroom equipment that you could think of. She was almost as well equipped as a hospital. There were special pans for both ends, and stools, and a bed that went up and down at the push of a button. Aunt Myrtle had a grand collection of all sorts of medical care items, stuff to cover just about any illness or emergency. Special shelves with everything from ace bandages to band aids were behind the small closet doors in Aunt Myrtle's bedroom.

The sad part of it all, Mary reflected, was that Aunt Myrtle hadn't had any good times for years. She had crippled herself with illness and fear. She had always said no to invitations that sounded like great fun because she was afraid she would get ill, or catch something in the crowd. She always said to Mary that "party food" made her ill, and it usually did.

Aunt Myrtle was loving, but demanding at the same time. She had been like a second mother to Mary ever since Mary was very small. Mary's own mother died shortly after Mary was born. As the time passed, and as Mary became a young lady, it seemed their roles reversed as Aunt Myrtle needed the care, and Mary became the caretaker.

Aunt Myrtle's condition left Mary with very little time for herself. There was no time to make friends and have the fun that others enjoyed. For instance, Mary had planned to go skiing this week-end, but with Aunt Myrtle in bed with no one to take care of her, Mary felt that it was her responsibility to take charge. There was the housekeeper, Mrs. Hanley, but she had to have time off just like anyone else. Another fun weekend down the drain.

Mary attended Jr. College and was working for grades that would be good enough so that she could enter the nursing program. She really wasn't too worried, as her grades were excellent, but she would be a little concerned until the program was in her pocket. Aunt Myrtle's illnesses had taught Mary a great deal about nursing and care giving.

Mary lived in a lovely home with her father. Their house was not too far from Aunt Myrtle's. Mary's father would fuss at her to get out with people her own age and have a good time, but the studies, the housekeeping at home, and the caring for Aunt Myrtle did not leave Mary much time of her own for anything extra.

After hanging the phone back in its cradle, Mary called to her father as she started out the door. "Dinner's in the oven, Dad, I'm going to check on Aunt Myrtle. I may have to stay over again, I'll call you if I do." She heard her father mutter an answer as she hurried down the walk toward the street.

After seeing Aunt Myrtle's pathetic condition Mary called her father to say she would not be home. She wanted to be able to keep an eye on her through the night. Then she called her friends and cancelled her ski trip. This really hurt, but she had only one Aunt Myrtle, and there would always be ski trips.

Mary set about straightening Aunt Myrtle's bed and plumping the pillows behind her Aunt's back.

"Thank you, dear," said Aunt Myrtle exhibiting weakness as Mary dusted and set the room in order.

"No one wants to be sick in a messy room,"sh e thought to herself as she folded the big comforter on the end of the bed. Mary made a mental note to remind Mrs. Hanley, the housekeeper, to check on Aunt Myrtle's room before leaving at the end of the day.

Mary brought a pan of warm water and a washcloth to allow Aunt Myrtle to freshen up. Then she brought her a clean nightgown and helped her slip into it. By the time Mary was finished with her "fussing" as Aunt Myrtle called it, the elderly lady looked real perky. "I checked the 'fridge' as I came in. Mrs. Hanley made some chicken soup and other goodies. Would you like some?" asked Mary.

"That would be wonderful," said Aunt Myrtle, "provided I have the strength to come downstairs"

"No, no," said Mary, "I'll bring a tray."

"Thank you, dear," sighed Aunt Myrtle, "and would you turn on the T.V. before you go downstairs?"

"Sure," smiled Mary. Then she hurried downstairs to fix a light supper for her aunt.

Mary prepared a lovely tray. There was soup, toasted homemade bread and butter. Mrs. Hanley had made apple butter for the toast and a bowl of jello for a sweet touch. As Mary brought the tray upstairs she could hear the laughter of the T.V. audience along with ——surprise—--the giggles of Aunt Myrtle. As Mary entered the room Aunt Myrtle's smile faded and she settled back on her pillows to be the patient.

Mary was ashamed of herself as she felt a twinge of resentment. "I think maybe she's not as sick as I thought she was," Mary said to herself.

Mary watched as Aunt Myrtle downed every crumb on the tray. As her aunt daintily dabbed at her lips with the pale blue napkin, Mary gathered up the dishes on a tray and took everything downstairs. There she washed and dried the dishes and cleaned up the kitchen.

When Mary went back upstairs Aunt Myrtle asked for a glass of water. "I must take my pills," she said. Mary watched, she could not believe her eyes, she was fascinated with this procedure. Two red pills for this, one pink for that, two blue for this, four white for that, Mary lost track as Aunt Myrtle downed one pill right after the other.

"Well, Aunt Myrtle, you seem pretty well taken care of, I guess that, I could go—"

Aunt Myrtle stopped her, "I'm afraid to stay alone Mary. I'm not sure I wouldn't have some sort of attack."

All right then", said Mary. "Just relax, I'm planning to stay right here.

"Good!" said Aunt Myrtle, settling back on her pillows. Mary watched as Aunt Myrtle's eyes became heavy, and soon she was fast asleep with a trace of a smile on her face.

Mary sat in the rocker and absentmindedly rocked as she listened to the even breathing of her aunt. Then she whispered to no one in particular, "Oh, Aunt Myrtle, please get well so that you can be happy."

"She is happy," said a voice.

"Who said that!" demanded Mary, becoming wide awake now.

"I did, me, Illch, that's who." Mary looked in disbelief at an ugly little creature with big ears, and a thermometer hanging from his lips like a wet cigar. He was sitting on the end of Aunt Myrtle's bed, feet dangling over the side. Mary was so surprised she could only gasp.

How dare you say that, Mr. Inch."

"Illch," corrected the little creature.

"How dare you say that Mr. Illch," said Mary. Aunt Myrtle has suffered for years.".

"Mary, Mary, Mary," said Illch, slowly shaking his head from side to side. "Aunt Myrtle is happy when she is sick. She doesn't realize this, of course, but she could change a lot of things for herself."

"Like how?" said Mary defensively.

"By imagining herself whole, well, healthy, and glowing with well being," said Illch.

"How is she going to do that when she feels so awful?" asked Mary.

"It's called Imagineering, Mary. You can imagine and fantasize anything you want. Illness has its beginnings deep inside our being. Many times we can outwit disease simply by 'seeing' ourselves well. Now, Aunt Myrtle has no one in this world outside of you and your father. She loves you, Mary, as you are the center of her narrow world. The only way she is sure of love and caring is when she is ill. I'm not saying that she is faking it, but she does seem to become sick on cue. Don't judge her for this, she is not aware of it. Do you understand what I'm trying to say? You are enabling her to be sick." Illch was smiling tenderly at Mary, this was such a hard thing to have to tell her.

"Oh no," said Mary. "That means that I'm helping her to be sick, that's awful, but what do I do about it? I love her very much, but I want to have a life of my own, too. Every trip or party that I have planned in the past six months I have had to cancel because Aunt Myrtle is ill. I feel guilty when I resent her for this, but it's hard to give up all my activities for her. What can I do? I don't want to hurt her, she was there for me when I was little and needed her."

"Would you like me to help? I've handled many cases like this before. Please, Mary, trust me. I can make a difference."

"This is all a dream," said Mary. "so I guess that it's OK if I trust you. What have I got to lose?" She got up then and went to her own room across the hall, left the door open a bit in case she was needed. Quietly she slipped out of her clothes, into her night clothes and into bed. In no time she was sound asleep.

Aunt Myrtle stirred in her sleep, and half awake she felt something tweak her toe. "What in the world?" she said, and then she sat up in bed, flipped on the low bedside lamp and just stared. "What and who are you? Where do you come from? You look absolutely dreadful, do you know that?" She was looking with disbelief at Illch sitting cross legged at the end of the bed. They both looked at each other for a few minutes. Illch was the first to speak.

"You look pretty dreadful yourself," he said, which caused Aunt Myrtle's jaw to drop. "To answer your question, my name is Illch. I have come to help you get out of this sick bed, and into the fun of living the rest of your life. I also would like to ease things for Mary so that she can have a life of her own."

"What do you mean?' asked Aunt Myrtle.

"My job," said Illch, "is to help people get well. If I'm needed, then I take over the sickness for people so all thought and consideration of any sickness can be forgotten."

Illch moved closer to Aunt Myrtle and took her hand. "Look at yourself in the mirror. Pretty awful right?" Aunt Myrtle shuddered at her own reflection.

"Look beyond the reflection that you see, and you will see another you that is the way you would like to be," said Illch enthusiastically. "Practice it every day and you'll see the change come about. Haven't you ever heard that fairy tales can come true, it can happen to you?"

"A lot of good that does me," said Aunt Myrtle, "how can I be young at heart when my body is old and sick?"

Illch ignored her question and looked at her bedside table. "How many of those pills do you take?" he asked.

"I take them all!" said Aunt Myrtle proudly. "I take them all faithfully every day, and have for years." Aunt Myrtle gave Illch a smug look.

"When is the last time you took this list to the doctor to see if it's all right for you to be taking all these pills?" asked Illch.

"I have never done that. It would be insulting to Dr. Linder. Besides he knows what I take, he prescribed them all." said Aunt Myrtle.

"So do you think that he is really aware of just what you are taking with all the patients that he has to take care of? It is my guess that a good part of your sickness is too many pills," said Illch.

"You don't know that to be true. Why, I've been taking these pills for years."

Illch changed the subject. "How much water do you drink?"

Aunt Myrtle was getting very irritated. "I don't know exactly, at least a couple of big glasses a day.

"That's not enough," said Illch. "You need at least eight glasses a day to keep healthy."

There was a long silence, and then Aunt Myrtle looked squarely at Illch and said, "Why should you care about me?"

"We're supposed to care about each other, " he said. He went on "And then there's Mary, she spends a lot of time here taking care of you. She needs a little more freedom to do the things that young people enjoy. Don't you love her?"

"Love her?" exclaimed Aunt Myrtle, "Mary is my life, my heart, my world."

"Well it's time that you got a heart and life and world of your own," said Illch gruffly.

Aunt Myrtle's face was red with rage. "How dare you pick on me when I'm so ill," she said tearfully.

I'm not picking on you, I'm wanting to help. Tomorrow get out of that bed and let me get in, steady your legs and hold up your chin. You see, the idea is that I will be sick for you. Make an appointment to see the doctor and check out the pills. Start with the water right away, it's a cheap way to start the healing. Water washes out the insides, just as soap and water cleanses the outside of the body. Also, get out and walk and walk and walk. I'll help, but you have to take things into your own hands and help yourself."

Nothing more was said. Finally Aunt Myrtle said to herself, "This has got to be the craziest dream I have ever had. What in the world could I have eaten to bring it all on?" She turned over on her side, switched off the light and muttered to herself. "I know one thing, I've got to get some sleep."

The next morning as Mary busied herself in the kitchen, she was surprised to look up and see Aunt Myrtle standing in the doorway.

When Mary saw her standing there, she rushed to her side and said, "Oh Aunt Myrtle, are you O.K.? Do you think you should be up?"

Aunt Myrtle smiled, pulled out a kitchen chair and sat down. "I'd like a cup of coffee Mary, have you made any?"

"I sure have," said Mary. "Here, let me get you a cup." Mary went to the cupboard and took out two china cups and filled them with freshly brewed coffee. "Here you go," she said, handing the coffee to Aunt Myrtle. "I'm so happy to see you up this morning. You must be feeling better."

"How I feel really hasn't much to do with anything," said Aunt Myrtle, to Mary's surprise. "It has suddenly occurred to me that it's not so much how you feel, as how you think you feel. Does that sound a little crazy?"

Mary looked at her aunt, bewildered. "I'm not sure. Exactly what are you trying to say?"

"I had a funny dream last night," said Aunt Myrtle. "A strange little man came and sat on my bed and pinched my toe. He told me to check on my pills and to drink more water, and exercise. He held my hand and told me that instead of thinking myself sick all the time that I should start thinking myself well. Can you believe all that? What do you suppose it all means?"

"That's unreal, Aunt Myrtle. I'm sure you'd never be sick on purpose," said Mary, fighting to keep from smiling. "What do you think this dream means?"

"That's what I was asking you," said Aunt Myrtle. "From what the ugly little man said it means that I'm not trying hard enough to get better. Mary, did you know that I have not checked on my prescription drugs for a long, long time? I don't know if it's all right to be taking them all together or not. Some of them I got a long time ago, and others just recently. That could be the very thing that is making me sick."

"Oh, Aunt Myrtle you need to check that out, that could be dangerous." said Mary. "While I'm fixing breakfast get on the phone right now and make an appointment with Dr. Linder." Then Mary said, "Want some oatmeal?"

"That sounds wonderful," said Aunt Myrtle as she reached for the phone.

Aunt Myrtle made an appointment to see Dr. Linder the following Tuesday. As she ate her oatmeal and toast she talked to Mary about her illness. "You know Mary, I don't seem to be getting any better. But, on the positive side I don't seem to be getting any worse. I think I'll go upstairs and get dressed. Maybe I'll try and walk a little. Just down the street a little way. Would you come with me?"

"You know I will," answered Mary.

"Another thing dear, would you call the hairdresser for me? I took a long look at myself in the mirror before I came downstairs. It was frightening. I look like an old hag, like a discarded care package. I need a new hair-do and I need to fix myself up a little."

Mary was delighted with Aunt Myrtle's attitude. Mary knew her Aunt would feel better once she started to look better. Mary thought then about her own dream. Or was it a dream. Illch had said that Mary was enabling Aunt Myrtle to be sick. "From now on I'm going to enable Aunt Myrtle to be well," vowed Mary to herself.

Aunt Myrtle went to the doctor the following Tuesday. They made a day of it, she and Mary. First to the hairdresser, then to lunch and then on to Dr. Linder's office. Aunt Myrtle had made a list of all the things she was taking. Dr. Linder was very upset. "It's a wonder that you're as well as you are." He went down the list of prescriptions. Then he said "See me about this time next month." He handed Aunt Myrtle a prescription. "Take these, and flush the rest of those pills down the toilet. Also, remember to drink plenty of water." Aunt Myrtle nodded.

As they walked out the door of the doctor's office and started down the hall, a Mr. Winters, who lived across the street from Aunt Myrtle saw them. There was an enthusiastic greeting to both Mary and her aunt, then he said, "Myrtle you look wonderful. What have you been doing for yourself?"

Aunt Myrtle blushed and said a demure, "Thank you, Matthew, how nice of you to say so." Aunt Myrtle thought that Mr. Winters was just about the most attractive man she knew, but she was always sick, and Mr. Winters was the type that was always going places and doing things. He was not one to put up with people who enjoyed their so-called illnesses.

"Maybe I could call you later, Myrtle, would that be all right? he asked.

"I'd like that," smiled Aunt Myrtle.

When they got home, Aunt Myrtle said to Mary. "Go on home, honey, not because I want you to, but because you need some time for yourself. I'll be all right for now. Mrs. Hanley is here. If I need anything I'll call you."

All right," said Mary. "Now don't overdo. I will call you later. I love you," she called over her shoulder as she pulled away from the curb.

"I love you, too," she heard Aunt Myrtle call after her as she started down the street toward home.

Myrtle had had quite a day. "I'll take a little nap before supper," she said to Mrs. Hanley as she came by the kitchen. She went upstairs and opened the door to her room. She could not believe her eyes, she was dumbfounded!

There sat Illch in her bed, all covered up and looking absolutely awful. "I told you I'd be sick for you," he said. His eyes were puffy and watery, and he had a real green sick pallor. He coughed pitifully, then managed a weak smile. Then Aunt Myrtle blinked and he was gone.

She quietly closed the door, and went across the hall into the guest room. "I'm not getting back into that sick bed," she said to herself.

She removed her sweater and shoes, and sat down on the bed. Then she lay back on the soft pillows and pulled the lace coverlet over her. She was fast asleep in no time. "If there's illness in this house let Illch handle it. I have to get on with life," Aunt Myrtle said to herself just before drifting off to sleep.

WORNOG

An overstuffed worry can mess up your mind,
Take heart! There is help for the worrying kind.

Wornog's for worry, not you who is strained,
Cares are the subject for which he's been trained.

He lives in a tower, he's found there a lot,
Just worrying over his worry stew pot.

Gather your torments, your woes and despair,
And place them with Wornog, he's waiting up there.

All your concerns will be put in the stew,
He'll cook them away so they can't bother you.

Do it now! Stop the worry that's smothering you.
Your time for contentment is way overdue.

OLIVIA AND WORNOG

Olivia sat at her upstairs bedroom window, and holding back the lace curtains, she watched the scene across the street. The Taylor twins were busy packing to go on another outing. How Olivia envied them. They were always going someplace new and exciting. The back of the station wagon was open, and the girls, Lila and Lela, were packing it with all sorts of interesting and colorful equipment and luggage.

Olivia sighed as she watched them skip from the front door of the house to the back of the wagon. There was lots of laughter, chattering, and hustle and bustle. Olivia thought to herself, "Maybe I made a mistake turning down the twin's invitation to join them. The only thing is, it's going to be awfully hot where they are going, and I sunburn so easily. I would end up with a million freckles. What if there were snakes, and stinging bugs, and heaven knows what else? I guess it's a good thing that I'm not going. I do have to admit though, it would have been nice to sit around the campfire after dark. They'll roast hot dogs and marshmallows and sing funny songs. But there're always mosquitos to spoil the fun, and I do worry around campfires." Olivia really wanted to go with them, but she worried about every detail. She just couldn't let herself have any fun.

The twins piled into the car and soon everything was loaded, and everyone was ready to go. Lila looked up at Olivia's window and smiled and waved goodbye. "It's going to be a lonely place around here without those two nuts,." she smiled wistfully to herself. A tear rolled down her cheek as she watched the car disappear down the street and around the corner. "What will I do with myself all this week," she pondered.

Suddenly Olivia was startled out of her sad thoughts with the ringing of the telephone. She bounced up and skipped across the room to answer. "Hello, this is Olivia speaking," she said.

Hi, Olivia," said a voice on the other end of the line. "It's me, Susie. Wanna come down to the park with me? There's going to be a high school group practicing for their cheerleading team. Bridget is going to be there, maybe we could learn a few pointers." The girls knew Bridget through her little sister, Jenny.

Susie, Olivia's friend lived down the street and around the corner. Olivia, the twins, Jenny, and Susie had talked of trying out for the Jr. High cheerleading squad. Olivia hesitated. "Gee, Susie, I ought to go over my homework again."

"I thought you said you had finished your homework," Susie sounded disappointed.

"I usually go over it several times," said Olivia. "I'm always afraid that I left out something, or misspelled a word, or did something wrong. I worry—"

Susie cut her off, "Gosh, Olivia, you always worry about something. Tell me, is there anything that you don't worry about?"

"Never mind," said Olivia, "I'm just being cautious."

"Look," said Susie, "we'll only be a little while, and you have until a week from Monday to get your assignments in. Come on, Olivia, don't be such an Anxiety Annie."

"Well," stammered Olivia," wait until I tell Mom, and I'll have to get a sweater, it could turn cold later on."

Susie giggled, "Yes, do bring a sweater, and your umbrella too, it might rain."

"Oh gosh, do you think it might?" exclaimed Olivia.

"No, worry wart, I was only teasing you," laughed Susie. "I'll meet you down at the corner in fifteen minutes. Bye."

After Susie hung up, Olivia raced downstairs toward the kitchen. Mrs. Leland looked up and smiled, "What's all the excitement about?"

She was happy to see Olivia acting enthusiastic about something

"Susie wants me to go down to the park with her to watch the high school cheerleading squad. Is it OK, Mom?" Olivia asked.

Mrs. Leland said, "It's all right, but don't be gone longer than a couple of hours, as we're having an early supper, remember?" She was happy to see that Olivia was getting out, as she felt Olivia spent far too much time in her room.

"See you later, Mom," Olivia called over her shoulder as she hurried out the front door. Mrs. Leland heard Olivia's voice trail off as she ran down toward the corner. "I'll see you in a couple of hours."

"It's good to see her going out for a little fun," thought Mrs. Leland. "She's such a homebody, and she's so fretful."

When Olivia reached the corner she looked both ways, no Susie. She looked at her watch, started to pace and checked both ways again, and wondered. "Sue should be here by now. It's been at least seventeen minutes since we talked." Olivia frowned, "Where is she? Where could she be? I sure hope nothing has happened to her, I hope she's —" Olivia's scary thoughts were interrupted by Susie's voice behind her.

"Hi, Olivia, come on, this is going to be fun. I brought a notebook to take some notes on the stuff they are going to be doing, and a camera just in case."

"Gosh, Susie, I was worried, you were late. When you didn't get here right on time I was afraid that something had happened. I was so worried!"

"Oh, Olivia, of course you were," said Susie, "You always are."

"Now Susie, you stop that!" cried Olivia.

The two of them headed for the park, laughing, planning and just making small talk. It was a perfect day, sunny with just a few puffy clouds sailing overhead.

When they reached the park, they found a pleasant grassy spot under a big oak, and both girls settled themselves down comfortably. They had a wonderful view of what was going to be happening. Both girls were taking in everything. There was a special way of setting up, and Susie's pencil was busy taking notes on everything and her camera was recording pictures of each exercise. Suddenly they heard a voice behind them.

"What are you two doing here?" It was Bridget.

"We're here to watch the high school cheerleaders to see if we can pick up any pointers. We're going to try out for the Jr. High squad," said Susie.

"Great! Let me know if you have any questions, and I'll help all I can. I also have some group instructions that I can share too. Gotta go now." And with that, Bridget joined the rest of the high school group.

The whole high school team was really quite good. They had flips, cartwheels, and clever pom-pom demonstrations, along with well-executed dance steps. The best part of all was the grand finale when they did the pyramids. Susie and Olivia were mesmerized. They took in every little detail, and stayed until the whole practice was over.

As they left the park Bridget joined them again. "Well, what do you think?" she asked. "Did we pass?""

"You were wonderful," said Olivia, "I loved it all."

"I loved the pyramids," said Susie. "We're going to do some of those tricks."

"I have some group instructions sheets I can let you use," said Bridget.

"Thanks a lot, these will be a great help," said Susie. "Heaven knows we need all the help we can get. We'll let you know if we need any thing else in the way of assistance. Be sure and say 'hi' to Jenny, and tell her we'll be counting on her, too."

As the girls made their way home, they chatted about moves, routines, and of course, costumes. Susie commented, "You know, the pyramid routines were wonderful, Olivia."

"Yes, but they were scary," Olivia observed.

Susie ignored the remark. "Let's see, Jenny, Alice, Meg and Shirley could do the bottom, the twins and I could do the second row, we'll need two more for the third row, and you Olivia, you can do the top. You're the smallest, and would be the lightest to hold up in the air."

Olivia looked at her horrified. "Me? Hold me up in the air? Don't be crazy, why, I'd be scared to death. It's not so easy, I could fall you know. I might break something, like my neck, or a leg or—. I just couldn't. Trust me, I'd worry the whole time."

"Don't be silly," said Susie. "Mrs. Wright will help us during gym period. She knows all the safety precautions, and knows how to set up routines so that no one can get hurt."

Olivia looked doubtful. "But Susie, you know how I worry, I just don't know if I could get up the nerve to do it.

Susie looked at her with disgust. "Oh, for goodness sake Olivia, you're a real pain. I'm your friend, and for that reason I'm going to tell you exactly the way it is."

"The way what is?" said Olivia.

"All of us are getting pretty sick of putting up with your worry about this, and your worry about that. You're starting to be a real drag, a gigantic damper." Susie turned and looked squarely at Olivia, "You find reasons to keep from doing anything and everything because you worry and fret whether it's necessary or not. You really aren't much fun anymore. I'm sorry Olivia, we all like you very much, but we don't like to always listen to your unfounded pessimism."

Olivia hung her head. "I'm sorry, Sue, it's just that I'm always afraid that—"

Susie interrupted, "That's right, Olivia, you're always afraid and you always worry, and we're tired of hearing about it!"

They had reached the front of Olivia's house. Susie went on. "Look, all of us, the twins, and I, and the others, we all want to do this cheerleading squad thing. If you can't overcome your fear problem, we can find someone else to replace you, it's just that simple." Susie whirled around and before Olivia could say anything, she was halfway down the street, and Olivia was standing there alone.

Olivia looked after her as the tears welled up in her eyes and rolled down her cheeks. "They just don't understand," she thought, "I really am afraid, and I really do worry, all the time, it's just the way I am, I wish I could be different."

As Olivia opened the screen door she could hear her mother in the back of the house. "I'm home, Mom," she called.

"How was it?" asked her mother, "Did you have fun?"

"Sure did," called out Olivia, then to herself she thought, "About as much fun as usual." She didn't want her mother to see the tears in her eyes nor the hurt on her face.

Olivia went through the house out the back door into the garden. The big hammock under the maple tree in the back offered her a safe and quiet retreat, a place where she could ponder what had happened, and try to figure out what was wrong with her. "The other girls don't worry," she mused. "What's the matter with me? How come I worry about everything?" She laid back, her hands clasped behind her head, and looked up. The clouds overhead were changing into pictures. "Yes," she thought, "there's a fish, an airplane, maybe an angel." Suddenly the cloud watch came to an abrupt halt. Olivia heard a loud "Pop" and then she heard someone clearing his throat—-.

"Ahem."

Olivia looked over her shoulder, and then she sat upright, almost falling out of the hammock. She gazed in amazement. There, in the garden, leaning against the big rock by the zinnias was a little man-like creature. Olivia thought to herself, "I'm imagining this, gosh that's great, now I'm seeing things too. Poor little creature, he sure is ugly, and he looks so worried. Then she said out loud. "Whatever are you, and where did you come from?"

The little creature came closer to her and managed a smile. "I'm Wornog, and I don't come from, I just appear when I'm needed or when you call for me out loud. Olivia, you need me desperately, if I may say so." He looked very serious then and said, "Do you have any idea how many times you say, 'I'm afraid', or 'what if', or 'I worry about?' Look my dear, sometimes worry is just impractical."

Olivia blinked at him. "Just what do you know about worries?" Then to herself, "I don't believe this is happening to me."

He answered her, "I'm Wornog. I live in a tower. I'm found there a lot, just worrying over my worry stew pot."

"So?" said Olivia.

"So you give me your worry, it's put in the stew, where it's all cooked away so it can't bother you," said Wornog.

Olivia frowned and said "That's easy for you to say."

"Look, Olivia," said Wornog, "I'm here to help. I know that you want to do things with your friends, but your worry and fear and lack of self trust are keeping you from having any fun at all."

Olivia hung her head. "I know it, but how can I change the way I am?"

"You can do it several different ways." Wornog expressed a little smile, "Number one, take precautions. Number two, always be prepared for where you're going and what you are going to do, then go on and have a good time. Don't be afraid to experience new things, experience the thrill of adventure. Worry can cause you to become a cripple, unable to go anywhere or do anything. Preparation is the key word. Then you gotta learn to trust yourself. If you're scared of something, find out more about it. It most likely isn't scary at all. List what's good and what's bad, and then learn to cope with the bad part."

"That sounds great," said Olivia, "But how do I cope with the worry?"

Wornog looked at her and said, "You give the worry to me so that I can cook it away." Wornog went on, "Find out as much as you can about your worry. If it's something you can fix, fix it. If there's something you don't understand, ask questions, learn about it, research it. Once something is out in the open, it's not so scary anymore. There was a wise man who once said, 'the only real fear we have is fear itself.'"

"You see, Olivia, worry can make you an invalid, and in the end it solves nothing!"

Olivia looked at him doubtfully. "It sounds good, but is it practical, will it really work?"

Wornog winked at her. "It will if you give it a chance. Do things the best that you can. Take precautions, be prepared, whatever you do or want to do, keep your wits about you. Most of all, please understand that worry has no power over you except the power you give it. Take all this in stride and then go on and have fun, and enjoy life. If you really get in a bind, call me."

"Call you..........? Call you where?" asked Olivia.

"Anywhere, anytime. Just say 'Wornog' out loud, and I'll appear with a 'Pop' to gather your worries to take them away. OK? Deal?" Wornog was grinning at Olivia and was nodding his head.

"Deal," said Olivia, finding it hard to accept that this was happening to her.

Olivia watched in surprise as Wornog waved, "See ya" and with a "Pop" he was gone. She laid back again in the hammock and pondered over what she had experienced. "I know that I imagined the whole thing," she thought," but it was so real, and so right." Olivia giggled to herself, "So—, I'll do some research on cheerleading, check out how it's done, how to approach it, what the dangers are, that kind of stuff." Olivia thought to herself, "and I was worrying what to do with my time while the twins were gone."

Olivia left the hammock, and headed for the house. She asked her mother, "Mom will you take me to the library after supper?"

Mrs. Leland smiled. "Of course, dear. There's something that I want to check on too."

Olivia went to the library and asked the librarian where the information regarding cheerleading could be found. She found the books that she needed. All the important information on safety, and how to avoid getting hurt. Olivia made lots of notes, and suddenly the whole idea of being on top of a pyramid seemed like fun, and certainly nothing to be afraid of. She smiled to herself. "Just wait until Susie sees how much information I was able to gather. Replace me? I think not!"

The next morning Olivia awakened to a beautiful sunny day. She threw up the shades, opened the window and breathed in deeply. "That air is great," she thought to herself. Olivia turned on the shower tap, and relished the warm water on her body, and the sweet smell of soap on her skin. "What a day," she mused, "What a wonderful beautiful day." While Olivia dressed she thought of all the great things she had learned at the library, and from Wornog, and how to put them to good use. "I can't wait to share with Susie what I have found out. Wait until she hears all the ideas that just popped into my head. Wow, did I ever sleep well." Olivia finished dressing and hurried downstairs.

"Hi, you two wonderful people," Olivia said to her parents. "Isn't this the most glorious day of all times?" Mr. Leland looked at his wife in surprise. Their eyebrows disappeared into their hairlines.

Olivia lifted the lid from the pan on the stove, sniffed and said "Ummm, sausage and onion omelet with cheese! I could eat a horse!"

"I thought that particular omelet gave you indigestion," said Mrs. Leland, "I only made enough for your Dad." Then she asked, " Would you like some too?"

"Would I," said Olivia, "You can say that again, and Mom, I've outgrown all that indigestion stuff."

Olivia ate a hearty breakfast. Feeling like gangbusters, she went up to her room to clean up and make her bed. She looked around, and satisfied with what she saw, she reached for the phone. She smiled to herself as she dialed Sue's number.

She heard it ring and then heard a sleepy voice say, "Hello, Susie here."

"Hi Susie, it's me Olivia, can we get together"? I'd like to go over some ideas regarding the cheerleading squad."

Susie said with a groan, "Are you kidding? I thought you were ready to give all that up, besides, what time is it? Can't you sleep?"

"Now Susie, don't start," said Olivia good-naturedly, "Give me a chance."

"OK, Olivia," said Susie, "why don't you come over here since you're so bright eyed and bushy tailed. I'm just gonna have breakfast, but we can talk."

"OK, I'll be right over." Olivia waved goodbye to her parents as she announced where she was going.

Mr. and Mrs. Leland looked at each other, and Mr. Leland said, "What in the world has come over Olivia? I can't remember seeing her so, so—-up."

Mrs. Leland smiled, "I think it has something to do with the Jr. High cheerleading squad. I agree though, it is great to see Olivia so lively and enthusiastic"

Olivia headed straight down the street and around the corner. When she got to Susie's house she opened the gate, and walked up to the front door and reached for the knocker. She knocked several times, and finally Susie appeared at the front door, still in her robe, her hair all messy from sleep.

"What's all the commotion? How come the excitement? I thought it would take an earthquake to shake you up." Susie paused, "That was a joke Olivia."

Olivia ignored Susie's attempt at humor. She breathlessly began. "You know, Sue, after I got home I got to thinking about the team we'd like to put together. I sorta had a —well, a change of heart Anyway, I think I could manage the top of the pyramid."

"WOW." said Susie, "I guess you did have a change of heart. How come? What exactly did you do to change your mind?"

"For one thing," said Olivia, "I had no idea how bad my worry problem had become, and how irritating it was to others. I've discovered that all I have to do is say a magic word and the worry goes Poof and is gone."

Susie was sitting down to eat, "And the magic word is —?"

"I think that it's sorta secret," said Olivia, not wanting to tell Susie just how she came to the word "Wornog". She had tried just using the word with little concerns, and it worked wonders. "You might call it Imagineering," Olivia said. "Just imagine the worry gone, use the word, and 'Poof' the worry goes."

"All right!" shouted Susie, "are you going to tell me the word or not?"

"Well, I guess it would be OK since we are such special friends. You were the one who helped me understand that I had a problem, so that I could do something about it. Brace yourself, the secret word is WORNOG."

"Wornog?" said Susie in surprise, "Where in the world did you get that weird word?"

"You might say it came to me," Olivia said with a half smile.

"And it works? asked Susie. "You say it works?"

"It works," said Olivia. All you have to do is just say it out loud and the worry's gone. I love it. I love the whole idea."

Olivia and Susie dug into the study of exciting and innovative cheerleading routines. They watched tapes of the Dallas Cowgirls and the Los Angeles Lovable Ewes. By the time the twins got home from their camping trip, they had most of their routines ready to practice, including the pyramid numbers.

A whole new thrilling world was opening up to Olivia. Because she had put aside her fear and worry, she was experiencing for the first time in a long while what being involved and having fun was all about.

They practiced to get their moves coordinated. They practiced to keep the routines flowing. They worked to be sure that everything was safe, and most of all nobody worried, they just had a good time, and it showed. Once in a while Susie or Olivia might whisper "Wornog" under their breath to get things back under control if they were anxious. It worked! They prepared themselves to be the best they could be, and they were! The rest of the team were really impressed, and delighted in what Olivia and Susie had worked out. They were very happy to find out that Olivia had made some changes in her inner attitude and her thinking, and was now "ready for anything."

By the time school opened again, their whole act and workout was ready. The try-outs were Tuesday after school. All of the final team were committed to being the best they could be. They had practiced until their muscles were sore. Each one had on a red skirt, a white sweater, and white socks and saddle shoes. They had made red and white pom poms and they all looked quite professional.

As Olivia smiled down from on top of the pyramid, she looked over towards the door. Something caught her eye. On top of the Exit sign she noticed a familiar little gnome-like figure. Wornog sat there, his whole face lit up with a big smile. He winked at Olivia then made a "V" for victory sign with both hands. Olivia waved, then "POP" he was gone.

You probably wonder if Olivia ever worried again. Well, she occasionally became concerned about things. When she did, she tackled the task of finding out what was wrong, and set about to fix it. She thought of Wornog often and how much peace he had given her. Although she thought about him, she only called him in an emergency. She owed him so much—a whole new life without worry!

"There are so many others out there that he needs to help," sighed Olivia. "I can be concerned, and that's O.K., but I need never really to worry about anything again."

CLUNERGEN

Decision can cause a great deal of depression,
And yet must be made with the utmost discretion.

No slide rule or chart can make up your mind,
Clunergen decides for the hesitant kind.

His tent is a place where he'll make your decision,
His scale will weigh doubts with careful precision.

All questions have answers, so make this your test,
Give it thought and then ask, "Is this really my best?"

Make up your mind with good Clunergen's aid,
Follow your plan and don't be afraid.

How will you know the way to decide?
The path that is right gives you comfort inside.

ANDREA AND CLUNERGEN

When Andrea put the finishing touches on her makeup that morning, she was muttering to herself, "Why am I like this anyway? Other people aren't like I am, it's so hard for me to decide, why oh why can't I make up my mind? This whole year has been nothing but one frustrating thing after another." She sat down in front of the mirror and put her hands over her face.

Andrea pondered there for a while, unhappy with the world in general and what she was feeling about herself. Then she separated her fingers and peeked out at her image in the mirror. "Maybe I should change my hair color," she thought to herself. "Forget it," she mused, "I'd never be able to make up my mind about shades, and I'd probably end up with green hair or something awful."

"Well, let's see, should I wear the purple sweater, or the fuchsia?" Andrea tried both colors next to her face and considered. "Oh, I don't know. Eenie Meenie Minie Moe, there, purple it is." Andrea got up out of her seat abruptly, "I can't think about things now, I'll go nuts," she thought to herself. She grabbed her purple sweater, crossed the room, and hurried downstairs to breakfast and the wonderful aroma of bacon and eggs. Mrs. Allen was just putting the food on the table. She looked up as Andrea entered the room.

"Hello, dear, breakfast is ready. Come and sit down." She put Andrea's plate down and then sat down beside her. "Andrea dear, have you gone by to finalize the choice for your senior pictures?"

Andrea rolled her eyes in frustration. "No, Mom, I can't make up my mind which one to choose. Please don't bug me while I'm eating," she said between mouthfuls.

"There are the three that I like," said Mrs. Allen, ignoring Andrea's remark. "Any one of those three poses would be lovely."

"I know, Mom, but which one?" Andrea frowned. She knew she had only a couple of days left to make her decision. If she waited any longer her picture could not be included in the yearbook. "I'll go by this afternoon and make a final choice. I'll just have to make some sort of selection and like it or not, that's it. I'm running out of time." Andrea smiled at her Mom, stood up abruptly, and said "I'm going to meet Mim in fifteen minutes so I gotta go." She picked up her school books and started out the door, then paused and looked back at her mother. "I have to stop and decide on the dress for the graduation ball on Saturday. I might be a little late, so don't worry."

"Oh Andrea," said Mrs. Allen," haven't you done that yet? Your dress will have to be altered in the waist and at the hemline. You don't have much time, I hope you have a dress in mind."

"Oh, I do," said Andrea," I just have to decide which color. It comes in "blue, aqua, pink, and lavender. Mim's going with me, so that'll help. Bye Mom, see you later." With that Andrea was out the door and down the walk on her way to school. "End of discussion." she said to herself.

Senior year in highschool was really giving Andrea fits. She had always been slow with making up her mind, and this year it seemed like there was one big decision factor after another. She agonized over every situation, sometimes for weeks. She would weigh the pros and cons, adding up one list and then another. She worried and fretted and stewed over every course of action, and sometimes the very thought of it all fatigued her beyond understanding. Andrea had absolutely no confidence in her choices.

Andrea thought about these things as she walked to meet Mim. When she reached the corner where they were to meet, she dropped herself gratefully upon the bus bench. "I'll sure be glad when this is all over with," she thought to herself. "But then I suppose there will be something else to come along that I will have to make up my mind about."

Graduation is a flurry of activities for students in their senior year. There's a decision about the class ring. Then who is a "must" for signing the yearbook. Oh dear, there were three invitations to the graduation ball. It took her three weeks to decide on Bill, and then she still wasn't really sure about her choice. Then there were the senior pictures. There must have been twenty poses to choose from. Selections had to be made regarding the announcements, and who she would send them to. She had yet to decide on the ball gown and whether shoes will be high heels or low. "Low," she suddenly decided. "Bill is a little short, and I'd hate to turn out taller than he is. It really doesn't matter that much, Bill is a real terrific person." So low heels it was. Besides most of the girls would have their shoes off by the end of the evening anyway.

Suddenly Andrea heard Mim's cheerful "Hello my friend" from behind her. She turned to see Mim's light red hair shining in the morning sunlight. Her big bright million-dollar smile lit up her face.

"Hi," said Andrea. "Gosh Mim, you're always so, so "UP." Don't you ever fret about all the things we have to do this year and the choices we have to make? There must be a hundred or so different things to think about."

"No, I don't really worry, Andrea." Mim smiled at her, "I just run through it, then choose the best way I know how. Then I let it go from my thoughts and I don't worry any more about it. Somehow it always seems to turn out all right. Gosh, with all that is going on I'd be nuts if I didn't decide one way or another."

The girls walked the rest of the way to school without any special happening. Andrea was relating to Mim all she had to do to get ready for graduation. Mim stopped and looked seriously at Andrea.

"Now Andrea, you're going to have to sit down, concentrate and get with it. You have known that these decisions had to be made for some time now, and you've just been putting them off." Mim went on, "I'm your best friend, and I hate to see you stewing this way about things you can solve in a wink and put out of your mind. Really, Andrea, we have rehashed this over and over before, and it's all getting a little old. I'll see you at lunch, OK?" With that Mim turned and walked away toward her own classes leaving a perplexed Andrea standing alone.

Andrea felt a little rebuffed and dejectedly made her way toward study hall. It wasn't like Mim to turn her off. When she reached her seat she looked around. She was early and there was no one else around. She put her head on her desk, and felt the tears well up in her eyes. "Decisions are so scary, there's so little time and still I'm undecided," she thought to herself. Then all of a sudden there was a nudge at her elbow. When she lifted her head it was only to stare eyeball to eyeball into the eyes of an elfin creature with pointed ears sitting on her desk, with his legs dangling over the edge.

Andrea's jaw dropped in surprise. She jumped back and stared at the creature. "What in the world are you?" She glanced around her to see if anyone else was in the room watching all this. There was no one.

The funny little elf poked Andrea with his slide rule, and smiled lopsidedly. "It's about time you did something about your indecision. You're going to have to decide on things for the rest of your life. You might as well get used to it now. You're beating yourself to death by not making up your mind about the many things that are facing you. By the way, I'm Clunergen. Pronounced Cloo-nerg-gin. I'm going to help you Andrea."

"Just how are you going to do that?" Andrea couldn't believe that she was taking this whole thing seriously, talking back to this, this whatever he is.

"You'll see. You'll see how easy it is. Just trust me." Clunergen disappeared with a "pop" as some students entered the study hall. Andrea looked under and around her desk, but Clunergen was definitely gone.

"What are you looking for?" asked one of the students.

"Oh, I thought I dropped my pencil," Andrea said. Then to herself, "That has to be the craziest thing that ever happened to me in my whole life. Goodness knows though, I could use some help. Hope he's around when I decide on my senior pictures." Then she smiled to herself with her new secret, even if it was make believe.

When Andrea met Mim at lunchtime she had decided (all by herself) not to tell Mim about Clunergen. Besides, he'd be a little hard to explain. "She wouldn't believe it anyway," thought Andrea. Andrea said nothing negative all through lunch, and kept the conversation light. When they parted it was agreed that Mim would be joining her after school. They had to go to the photographer's studio, then on to the department store to decide on the gown for Saturday.

The bells on the photo studio door jingled as they entered. They walked toward the counter and the photographer's clerk came out from the back of the store.

"I'm here to pick up my proofs. I'll take them with me and decide tonight, all right? My Mom will bring back the one we go with and the others tomorrow. Is that OK?" said Andrea. "My name is Andrea Allen."

"Just a moment," said the clerk. She went to a cabinet and opened a folder with a bunch of envelopes. "Lets see, Allen, yes, here it is." She handed Andrea a slip of paper and said, "Just sign here."

Andrea signed the slip and then nudged Mim. "See, that wasn't so bad now was it?"

"Yes," said Mim, "But you didn't decide anything. I protest!"

"I will tonight. But I have to do it by myself. There are only three proofs to consider anyway, as the others are awful. Come on, lets go."

The girls got back on the bus and rode downtown to the Emporium. "I can't believe that we were at the photographers for less than five minutes," said Mim.

Andrea looked at her and smiled, "What you are seeing here my good friend is a new, assertive, assured, and decisive Andrea Allen."

"Wow, what has gotten into you anyway?" said Mim. "Have you found some sort of a fairy godmother or something?"

Andrea laughed, "Yes, or something."

When they arrived at the Emporium Andrea and Mim rode the elevator to the second floor. The ball gowns were over in the corner across the store, and the girls took their time getting over to where they were on display. All accessories, bags, gloves, shoes, jewelry, etc. were on that floor, and the girls took in everything as they passed. There were so many beautiful things to choose from. Andrea took a deep breath as they approached the gown department.

Andrea smiled at the clerk and said. "I'd like to try on that gown over there." She pointed to a gown on the mannequin.

"What color?" asked the clerk. "It comes in aqua, blue, pink, and lavender."

"I know," said Andrea, "but I haven't made up my mind yet as to color."

"Oh brother, here we go again," lamented Mim .

"Now Mim don't get in a snit. I'll decide easily, just you wait and see. Sit down right there and I'll model it for you."

Andrea took the blue gown from the clerk and headed for the dressing rooms. The clerk followed with the gowns in the other colors.

Andrea pulled the blue gown over her head and gazed at herself in the mirror.

"I think the pink would be better." Andrea nearly jumped out of her socks. There big as life sat Clunergen.

"My goodness, Clunergen, you scared me out of my wits. You said you'd help, now just why do you like the pink better? Or do you think possibly the aqua or lavender would—-"

Clunergen interrupted Andrea. "Definitely pink! Just hold each dress up to your face. You will notice that some colors will make your skin glow as the pink does, and others might make your complexion look sallow. Try the aqua and you'll see what I mean. Unless you're really hung up on one color, I'd say the pink will do the most for you. Check them all out Andrea and you'll see."

Clunergen was starting to tap his foot with impatience. "Come on now, decide for Pete's sake," said Clunergen. He fingered his chin while he watched Andrea try on all the gowns.

Finally, she spun around broke into a big smile and said, "It's the pink. You're right. It's great on me. Let's go with the pink. Oh this is great! I have made up mind in less than five minutes, and I'm sure that my decision is right." She zipped up the side of the gown, held up the hem of the skirt and swirled out of the dressing room like a movie star in an old T.V. commercial.

"This is it, Mim! This is definitely it. Just look at me, am I gorgeous or what?" Andrea turned and turned, and admired herself in the full length mirror.

Mim looked astonished. "You look beautiful in that color Andrea. Absolutely beautiful. I can't believe that you made up your mind on the first try, and so short a time. By the way, who were you talking to in there?"

"I was talking to myself, just to make sure I was doing the right thing. Like thinking out loud. What do you think? It has to be altered a little in the waist, and it's too long." Andrea beamed. It was such a load off her mind.

The clerk left and came back with the alteration lady. After Andrea was "pinned" she took the dress off and put her school clothes back on. Then she said to the clerk. "How soon can I pick this up? I need it for Saturday."

"Well, this is Monday, we can have it for you on Wednesday." said the clerk with a smile.

"Wonderful. Lets go home Mim, I have to hit the books for finals." said Andrea..

"Me too," said Mim. "But I have to tell you, Andrea, I have never, I mean never, seen you make up your mind so fast. What a change over the last time we went shopping. What a welcome change. Just what's going on anyway?"

Andrea beamed, "Oh, let's just say I'm getting a 'clue' about decision making, and not too soon either." She giggled at her own pun.

When Andrea got home she called out, "Mom I'm home."

Mrs. Allen came in the back door from the garden. "Well dear, how was your day? Did you get any shopping done, or should I ask?"

"Ask, Mom, Ask. You just won't believe it. I got my dress, and it's being altered. It's pink and you'll just love it." Andrea was breathless and bubbling over with excitement.

"Did Mim help you decide?" asked Mrs. Allen.

"No," said Andrea, "I decided all by myself with a little help from my fairy god person." Then she smiled.

"Oh Andrea that's wonderful" said Mrs. Allen, thinking that Andrea was only joking.

"Call me when supper is ready, Mom, I have to study. It's final time you know," said Andrea as she hurried upstairs, laughing all the way.

Andrea sat at her desk and opened a book to study. Then she heard, "Can we talk?" It was Clunergen sitting on her desk leaning against some book ends.

"Hi," said Andrea. "I was hoping you'd be here sometime this evening. I have to pick out my school pictures. Just a minute." Andrea dug into her purse. "Here, see? It's one of these three. What do you think?"

"Clunergen looked Andrea right in the eye and said, "It's not what I think, but what you think, Andrea that counts. If you really can't make up your mind, then spread out the three pictures and consider them carefully. Start a column under each picture. In each column list all the things you like about each picture. Then list all the things you don't like about each picture. The picture with the most plus marks wins. That's your choice!"

"You mean that it's just that simple to make decisions?" said Andrea.

"Yes, my friend, it's just that simple," answered Clunergen. "You have a good mind, Andrea, you have been fooled into not trusting the things you decide. #1, have a plan or idea of what you want or like. #2, establish a goal. #3, work toward that goal. Make your decisions upon the things that you have learned working for that goal. Does that make sense?"

"Can you explain it another way?" asked Andrea.

"Well, when you've studied a subject and have some idea how it works it should be easy to make changes and decisions regarding that subject." Clunergen smiled as he explained.

Clunergen went on. "When you made the decision about the ball gown you knew what style you wanted. When you really considered color it was easy to see which was right for you. Isn't that so?"

"That's so,"echoed Andrea.

"The best thing of all, Andrea, is when you have looked into something and know it well, your decision will be a comfortable one. And most of all if you do make a mistake, so what? Then it all becomes a valuable learning experience for the next time. See my point?" said Clunergen.

"Oh Clu," exclaimed Andrea." You are the greatest."

"No, Andrea, you are, and don't you forget it. Trust yourself, believe in yourself, be comfortable with yourself and your decisions. Y.ou are special. Consider this. There is only one set of fingerprints like yours. That makes you very important, you are one of a kind. You are perfectly capable of making a good choice. Know that, remember that, and trust that knowledge."

Clunergen smiled at Andrea, then said, "You'll be all right now. If not whisper my name and I'll be right with you. Help is just a whisper away. OK?"

"OK," said Andrea.

All through graduation week Andrea handled one difficult problem after another. What she learned was a feeling of self confidence, self respect, and self reliance. She got better and better, until it was easy." "What a difference, what a wonderful warm secure feeling," Andrea thought to herself.

Andrea received the respect and admiration of others, too. It was really just a matter of believing in herself. No more whining about deci-sions, no more making others wait while she agonized over some small choice.

After graduation there were college decisions. After college, job choices, and on and on. Andrea kept the wonderful things Clunergen had told her in her heart. The most wonderful thing of all was that Andrea, after all her choices, had peace of mind.

Andrea found that after every decision that was made, she could let it go knowing she had done best she knew how.

Life was definitely better and promised to be better still.

SKRINCH

Skrinch is a tightwad and has quite a load
Of boxes and bundles stuffed in his abode.

He never shares his abundance at all,
His bank account's big, but his feeling is small.

He grabs whatever is thrown to the side,
Be the item huge, tiny, tall, narrow, or wide.

There in his pocket he tucks things away,
It gets rather full, but he likes it that way.

It is greed if you keep what you really should lose.
Not need, if you keep what you never can use.

Giving's a gift that just giving can give.
Give Skrinch your greed and start in to live.

J. H. AND SKRINCH

The Marshall building was the tallest building in Century City. Forty-four-year-old J. Henry Marshall was the owner, founder, and Chairman of the Board. He was top man of the powerful international conglomerate known as J.H. Marshall Enterprises, Incorporated.

High up on the twenty-fourth floor J. Henry Marshall had his beautiful suite of offices. The inner office where he spent most of his time overlooked Los Angeles and Hollywood to the East, and on a clear day the ocean and Catalina Island to the Southwest. J.H. sat like a king on a throne in his enormous leather chair, and spread out before him was a mahogany desk that measured eight feet long, and five feet wide. The computer in front of him gave him instant control and information on all departments. His decision on any matter was final.

The office had a small but efficient well stocked kitchen adjacent to it and the studio bedroom arrangement was a place where he could have a snack, a complete meal, take a shower or a nap. Many times when J.H. worked late he stayed overnight in the building. Harold, his domestic right arm, was always there to take care of the mundane details of his life. It was Harold's duty to see to it that the refrigerator was well stocked with all of J.H.'s favorite foods, and to make sure that the bedroom was always ready in case it was needed. He took care of all the personal needs of J.H. while he was in the building. A complete wardrobe at the office was overseen by him too, so that J.H would always be ready for any occasion. There was a small exercise area with machines to help with fitness. J. Henry Marshall had it all, or at least most of it!

J.H. Marshall had been an orphan. He found out early in life that you had to work hard, and improve yourself to succeed. From the time he was fourteen years of age, he took care of himself, always planning and looking forward to the time when his efforts would make him a wealthy man. J.H. hated the idea of having to take charity. At the Orphanage they wore ill-fitting hand me down clothes and shoes, and at Christmas their toys were the discarded toys of other children. Early in his life J.H. promised himself that he would do anything to keep from ever taking charity again.

As a teenager and young man J.H. always had at least two jobs and spent most of his spare time at the library. He grew up before he had a chance to be a boy and had an uncanny understanding of the world of finance and business. By the time he was in his mid-thirties he was already a multi-millionaire, and was considered to be one of Los Angeles most eligible bachelors. Being in this most enviable position, he was literally besieged by beautiful and ambitious young women. He wasn't too interested in the ladies, there simply wasn't time. Now and then he would accompany a young woman to a concert or a dinner party, but most of the time he could be found dealing with the world of business from his "mahogany tower" as he called it. The world of finance seemed to be enough for him.

Miss Elders, his executive secretary, interrupted his reverie, "Mr. Marshall?" J.H. didn't answer right away as he was busy with some contracts. "Sir?" she asked. Miss Elders had been with J.H. since the building of the tower in Century City.

"Yes, what is it?" he mumbled, not looking up.

"Sir, we have several requests for donations. It is that time of the year," she smiled. "There's the Rescue Mission, very worthy I think, The Boy's Club, The Salvation Army, they all have had a shortage of funds this year due to many homeless persons that have no place to go. We have had our share of disasters too, what with the earthquake..."

J Henry cut her off. "You know how I feel about those bleeding heart charities. As I have said before, we'll always have the poor. It's beyond me how people can find themselves in such a mess, when there are so many opportunities everywhere. Nobody gave me any help when I was getting started, and I wouldn't have taken it if they had. People have forgotten the old 'bootstrap' way of getting ahead in the world. Establish a goal and go for it I say. Why, I started my building plans when I was just a lad, but then I think you've heard this story before."

"Yes, Sir, I have," replied Miss Elders with raised eyebrows. Then she thought to herself "The big cheapskate, those charities are really needy this year. He wouldn't even miss it." She started toward the door, turned, and looked at J. H. as she thought, "It really has nothing to do with all that, the only thing these people know is that they're cold and hungry." When he didn't look up she asked, "Will that be all, Sir?" Miss Elders waited at the door, but J.H. was deep in concentration.

"I'll be here until around eight-thirty," he said, "then I'm going home. I want to pack a few things for Tahoe. There's nothing like a week-end on the slopes to organize my thoughts on how to make my next ten million. That reminds me, call Harry and let him know I'll be needing the jet this evening. Oh, and Miss Elders, pick up a nice gift for Ted Lambert's little girl, It's her birthday, and I want him in a good mood for the board meeting on Tuesday. It's O.K. to spend up to a hundred bucks. She's a spoiled little brat and is used to getting expensive gifts. By the way, call Edward at my home and tell him to get my things ready to take to the lake."

"Yes, Sir," said Miss Elders, as she started to leave the room, she asked, "Will you be returning Sunday evening?"

"No, Monday around noon or there about..." he answered.

"Good night then, and have a good trip." And she was gone.

J. Henry Marshall dug into the pile of papers on his desk. It was almost nine o'clock when he finally looked at his watch. He didn't seem to notice when the first cough came from Skrinch. Then after a couple more ahems and coughs, J. H. saw him.

"Who are you? What in heck are you supposed to be?" J.H. surveyed the little man before him.

Skrinch sat on one of the chairs reserved for guests and glared at the tycoon. His long overcoat was bulging with money, and he had padlocks on his pockets. "I'm called Skrinch." he said "We need to talk."

"I'm imagining this and it will just go away," J.H. said to himself. He went over the last details of his paperwork, started to turn out the lights, and close the office.

"Not so fast mister," said the weird little man. "Not so fast. What are you going to do about those charities?"

"Just like I said, nothing! I'll say the same to you as I did to Miss Elders, they are not my responsibility. Besides, I don't think you're real, you're just evidence that I need a rest. Good night, I'm leaving." He called goodbye to Harold and left.

The building seemed to have an unsettling eerie silence as he rode his private elevator to the garage below. He unlocked the door, eased into the seat behind the wheel of his new Jaguar, belted himself in, and turned the key in the ignition. "Lock all the doors," he thought to himself, "never know who might be around these days."

J.H. waved as he passed through security, and went on out into the night. After driving a few blocks he felt a pulling on the steering wheel, as though he might have a flat tire. "Oh, don't tell me," he said to himself. He pulled over to the curb, and got out to check his tires. He didn't notice a van that had pulled over as well about a half a block behind him. Their lights were on dim and they were keeping a discreet distance behind. His right front tire was almost flat. He checked it out, walked back around the car to the driver's side, and reached in for his personal cellular phone. As he dialed the corporate garage for help, he walked back around the car to look at the tire. His attention was on the phone and the tire, and he didn't notice two young men get out of the van and move toward him.

As J.H. leaned over to check the tire once more, he sensed someone behind him, but it was too late. The blow came out of nowhere, and then there was total darkness.

The young men worked quickly, loading the unconscious J.H. into the back of the van, as one of them slid behind the wheel of the Jaguar. "I'll meet you guys at the warehouse." he yelled out the window as he hurriedly left the scene, low tire and all.

The men in the van smiled victoriously as they moved on down the street. The one in the back of the van guarding J.H., busied himself undressing his victim. As he took off the things that J.H. was wearing, he went through all the pockets and handed his belongings to the other two in the front. He seemed to be J.H.'s approximate size, so he took off his own clothes and put on J.H.'s. He dressed J.H. in his old blue jeans, tattered shirt, and jacket. The man looked down at himself and was pleased to see the clothes were a perfect fit. He tried the shoes, but they were too big.

The three men were delighted with the haul. They had all of J.H.'s credit cards, two thousand in cash, his jewelry, and expensive watch, plus the car.

Their plan had worked perfectly. Posing as service personnel they had entered the garage of the Marshall building and let most of the air out of J.H.'s tires. All they had to do is follow him until he got out to check his tires.

The driver of the van pulled over to the curb on a dark street. The men hurriedly hauled the limp body of J.H. out of the van and onto the sidewalk where they pulled it into a deserted doorway and dumped it. They ran back and jumped into the van and left, screeching their tires as they turned the corner to disappear into the night.

It wasn't long before J.H. heard a voice saying to him, "Wake up, wake up." He opened his eyes to look into the gaze of the funny little elf of a man with squinty eyes and bulging pockets without recognizing Skrinch.

"Who, or what, are you and what filthy place is this?"

"To answer your first question, my name is Skrinch. This filthy

place is where you landed when you got thrown out of a van by some men who were robbing you. I too was following you after the statement you gave to your secretary. After robbing you, the men in the van just pushed you out into the street and dumped you here, Are you hurt?"

"My head hurts a little, but other than that I guess I'm OK." J.H. rubbed the back of his head again. "What do you mean the statement I made to my secretary?" J.H. looked at his wrist and then back at Skrinch, "Where the heck is my watch?" He looked down at himself. "What? Where are my clothes? Where did I get these rags?"

"Well it looks as if Providence wants you to see how the other half lives," said Skrinch. "You see, sir, may I call you Sir"? Skrinch came closer, "Your secretary and I brought to your attention the fact that there are many hurting out there. You know yourself what it is to be one of the 'have nots.' It is easy to forget when we do well and have all we need, but we need to share with others or our wealth means nothing, or at least not as much."

"Wait a minute," interrupted J.H., ignoring what Skrinch was saying. "I need to make a phone call....let me see, wait a minute. I don't know who to call. I forget..Let me look in my wallet." He felt for his wallet. "My wallet,—it's gone." He started patting his pockets, "nothing, wait, these aren't my clothes."

"How do you know?" asked Skrinch, amused now at J.H.'s dilemma.

" I know, I don't know how I know, but I do, besides look at my shoes. You can tell by the shoes that these are not the clothes that go with them. But..." he rubbed his head again. "But who am I? I can't remember who or what I am. I know this is not me," he looks down at his clothes.

"Looks as if you're going to need a kind hand to help you out, doesn't it?" Skrinch was enjoying the panic that J.H. was experiencing. "Yes, it looks like you'll have to ask someone for assistance."

"You mean charity? I never have asked anyone, I never—well I mean I wouldn't," said J.H. sputtering.

"Are you hungry?" asked Skrinch.

Suddenly J.H. felt the hunger pangs in his stomach. "Boy, am I," he exclaimed.

"When did you eat last?" asked Skrinch.

"I don't know. I don't even know who I am." said J.H. "All I know is that I am hungry." It was almost eleven o'clock and J.H hadn't had anything to eat since lunch time. He was more than ready for a good meal.

"Then you'll be grateful for charity. It's always surprising how good, warm food humbles one."

"What's all this to you?" asked J.H.

"I'm Skrinch. It's my job to educate people like you. You need to learn that there's nothing wrong with taking charity once in a while, and there's nothing wrong with helping others when they need it. For example, I know a lot of millionaires who have more money than they could possibly spend, but they are afraid to spend it on anything except to make more money. Sometimes I wonder what happened to their self confidence. They made it once, so why couldn't they make it again? There's an old saying that if you cast your bread upon the water, it comes back with jam on it. t. It's O.K. to let people help you once in a while, it makes them feel good. It's also O.K. to help others when they need it, because that makes you feel good. Haven't you heard the expression to give until it feels good?"

J.H. said, "I've always believed that hard work and persistence pays off, not pie in the sky attitudes. In the meantime, wait....there's something going on in my head. Man, it sure hurts, and I don't remember who I am. But, as I said, I could sure eat!"

"Come on," said Skrinch. He lead J.H. down the street a couple of blocks and around the corner. There J.H. saw a dimly lit sign that read "Rescue Mission." He was cold, and his head hurt. He turned to say something to Skrinch, but he was gone.

"I knew I was imagining things," he said to himself. "I hope that bump on my head didn't make me any crazier than I already am."

J.H. hesitated at the door, rubbed a spot on the dirty glass and peered into a plain room with tables and chairs. He pushed open the worn, unpainted door, and was immediately grateful for the warmth inside.

"Welcome!" said a voice behind him, "How can we help?"

J.H. turned around and looked at a man who was wearing a frayed white shirt, a worn jacket, and well washed jeans. "I was told that I could get something to eat here, but if it's too late, I'll go. "He turned and started to go back out the door.

"Hey, not so fast, the man said, "don't go. We always have something to eat for the hungry, you're never too late. Come with me into the kitchen, we'll see what we can find. Our regular meals are served at 5:30, but we'll make an exception for you. My name is Brother Mel, what's yours? Just first name, if you want."

J.H. looked embarrassed, "You see, I had this blow on my head, and I can't remember my name. I wish I could."

Brother Mel turned to him, smiled and said, "If you need a place to sleep tonight, we can fix you up with a cot and a blanket. Not very fancy, but clean and warm. At least you'd be in out of the cold."

"I would be very grateful to stay until I get my head back together." J.H. smiled at his benefactor. "I'm tired, and I have a terrible headache."

"Maybe you'll feel better after you get some food in your belly," said Brother Mel.

J.H. enjoyed the hearty meal of stewed beef and vegetables. J.H. grinned and turned to look up at Brother Mel and said "How can I ever thank you enough, that was great."

'We'll think of something," said Brother Mel.

J.H. slept soundly, much to his surprise. His 6'1" frame hung over the end of the cot a little, but he was warm, and reasonably comfortable. Next morning after a shower and a shave, he was given a warm breakfast of oatmeal and toast. He looked for Brother Mel and found him in the Chapel dusting pews.

"Good morning " said Brother Mel. "What can I do for you?"

"The question is," said J.H. "what can I do for you? I would like to do something to earn my keep." Brother Mel smiled, and handed J.H. a broom. "Here, there's always room for one more on the clean-up around here." They worked without saying much, cleaning, sweeping, and dusting. When they finished Brother Mel said, "Well, we're not fancy, but we're clean! As my dear old mother used to say, cleanliness is next to Godliness."

When lunchtime came J.H. sat down at one of the tables and noticed a very attractive woman and a little girl sitting right across from him. The woman looked up, and then back down at her plate. The little girl stared at him and said, "Did you wash your hands?" She looked at him curiously.

"Yes, I did," said J.H. amused. " Is it OK if I start?

"Did you say Grace?" said the little girl, unsmiling,

"Well, not yet, is it OK if I say it to myself?" said J.H.

"It's OK with me she answered, "I hope it's OK with God. You know what? You look like."

Her mother nudged her and interrupted with, "Penny eat your lunch and don't bother the man."

"But Mom, he looks like—"

Her mother stopped her again "Penny, eat your lunch, and no more talking."

J.H. was overwhelmed with curiosity. "Pardon me, Maam," he said. "I can't help but wonder what a lady like yourself and your beautiful little girl are doing in a place like this?"

Penny's mother looked him right in the eye and said, "We're here to eat lunch. We ran out of money, and we got hungry. I had a good job until just a month ago when I was fired. Penny got sick, no job, no medical insurance. All we had went to pay the doctor and the pharmacy.

We had no money left for food, so here we are, not that it's any of your business."

J.H. couldn't help but notice what lovely brown eyes the mother had, just like the little girl's. "Where is your husband?" he asked.

"My Daddy is in heaven," the little girl volunteered.

"What happened with your job, if you don't mind my asking?" said J.H.

"My, you are the inquisitive one, aren't you? I worked in a large insurance office. There was this office manager who pushed himself at me. I told him that I wasn't interested, but he continued so I reported him. I got fired two days later."

"Where did you work?" asked J.H.

"At the Marshall building in Century City," she said.

"That name rings a bell," said J.H. His head started to hurt, and he saw flashing pictures of the building, his office, his apartment. J.H. held his head, "I wish I could get rid of this headache."

Penny couldn't stand it any longer, "Mommy, Mommy, he looks like the man in the newspaper. You know, the one that's lost."

"Oh, my God," said the woman. She looked at J.H., then at the news-paper, and emergency things "just in case." She readied Eddie's supper and said, "You'd better look at this yourself. Here." She handed him the paper she had taken from the bag she was carrying, and watched curiously.

J.H. unfolded the newspaper and started to read about his own dis-appearance. The article said that It was feared he had met with foul play, and asked people to call if they had any knowledge of his whereabouts. There was a reward of ten thousand dollars offered for any informa-tion on his disappearance. When he had finished reading the article, he smiled at Penny and her mother, "Well, you two, looks like you two have really helped me. Now I remember. I worked late in the office, drove off in my car and had a flat. I was hit on the head and the last thing I re-member was phoning the garage. They left me with little more than my dignity. Excuse me, would you? I need to make a phone call."

J.H. called his office and talked to Miss Elders She was happy to know he was all right, and said she would send a limo to pick him up.

J.H. went back into the dining room and smiled at Penny and her mother. "I have to get back Ms—just what is your name?"

"Its Susan, Susan Alexander."

Penny interrupted "What about the reward?"

"Penny!" exclaimed her mother. "Where are your manners?"

"She has a point Susan. It does look like you two are ten thousand dollars richer. I really don't know how to thank you. Is there somewhere I can call you later? I would like to take you ladies to dinner to have you help celebrate my return to the real world. Also I want to help with your job. Please report to personnel at the Marshall building as soon as possible. I will see to your job myself."

J.H. was excited that everything was working out so well. He was anxious to get into his own clothes and he scratched himself as he thought about the luxury of his own apartment and shower.

"Here," said Susan handing him the phone number and address. "I'm so glad all this had a happy ending for you. Thank you Mr. Marshall."

"Henry," he said, "my friends call me Henry. Goodbye ladies I'll see you soon. I'll call as soon as I can."

J.H. left then and walked to the waiting limousine outside the door. He looked back and waved at the new friends he had made. He unfolded the slip of paper that Susan had given him, looked at it and smiled.

The newspaper and TV reporters were at the Marshall building when he returned. He made a run for his private elevator just off the main hall because he didn't want the press to see him the way he was. He burst into his office with a whoop of excitement. "Miss Elders, where's Harold? Tell him I'm overdue for a shower and shave. Call the florist and have them send flowers and a certified check for ten thousand dollars to a Ms. Susan Alexander and Penny at the address here." he handed her the slip of paper that Susan had given him.

As J.H. was shaving, he smiled at his reflection in the mirror, pleased the way everything had turned out. Suddenly he was startled when he spotted Skrinch sitting on the lid of the commode behind him.

"All 's well that ends well," said Skrinch.

"What's that supposed to mean?" said J.H. laughing at the little creature.

"You'll send a donation of some kind to the shelter won't you?" asked Skrinch. "You saw first hand the job that the Rescue Mission is doing."

"I'll do better than that. I'm going to set up a trust for the various charities that you and Miss Elders are so concerned about. My attorneys can arrange it so that each one will receive a set sum every month, this way it will be income they can depend on. You're right Skrinch, helping others makes me feel good."

Skrinch grinned, "It's a beginning, J.H., yes, it's a beginning."

J.H.'s life was a whole new world, as he became involved in the activities to help the unfortunate. It seemed like the more he did for others, the more exciting his life became.

As for Penny and her mother, they became a permanent part of J.H.'s life, enriching his world even more. Skrinch appeared when no one was around to see how things were going, but after a while he came no more, as he was very busy with so much work to do. There were many more lives to enrich.

J.H. said one morning to Penny and Susan, "I wish I could reward those guys that robbed me. If it hadn't been for them, I would never have found the two of you, nor would I have such a happy life. Miss Elders now thinks I can do no wrong, but we all know different." They all laughed together with agreement.

PRILLDIM

Prilldim's the guy who has the tradition
Of helping the fellow without inhibition.

If blabbing's your problem, that's way out of place,
Sound off to Prilldim and save a red face.

He sits in a corner with hands folded neat,
And powders your rashness when you want to bleat.

When others who love you are put on the spot,
Your "no inhibitions " will hurt them a lot.

You're out of control and do what's taboo,
The Prilldim can help what is troubling you.

You're "too much" -it's no wonder you're never invited.
When Prilldim takes over, you'll stop being slighted.

HARRY AND PRILLDIM

Harry Wurtz was probably one of the nicest fellows you could ever get to know. He was honest, kind, accommodating, and just plain helpful to everyone he came into contact with. Harry was a person who looked for things to do for others. He should have been the most popular guy in town. He should have been, but unfortunately, he wasn't, he wasn't at all!

Harry really tried, but always seemed to "mess up" in business and social situations. He always managed to "put his foot in it," when his intent was to be outgoing and helpful.

We all remember the time he jovially meant to pat a co-worker on the back for a job well done during a conference meeting. Unfortunately, his "slap on the back" was given with too much enthusiasm, and the dentures of the co-worker flew out of his mouth on to the conference table. The poor man was so embarrassed he resigned a short time later. Most of the office force blamed Harry for the resignation. The man had been a favorite, and a valuable asset to the company. The office force hated to lose him, and they all blamed Harry for the loss.

The sad part of it was that all Harry really wanted was to be accepted. He wanted to be "Joe Popular" and desired to be included in everything. He loved people and parties and gatherings where interesting things were debated and discussed. Unfortunately, after the first few times he didn't get invited again.

Harry decided he needed to change. He read the book on "Dressing the Young Executive" and began to be the fashion example to all he interacted with. He took the "How to Win Friends, Etc." course and really tried to apply it to the way he presented himself. But things only got worse. It seemed that every time he tried the situation would just work against him.

One of Harry's worst fiascos happened the time the company had its reception for the new Vice President. It was really a very posh affair. Black tie, and the ladies all seemed to have tried to outdo each other. Their gowns were incredible combinations of satins, laces, beaded chiffons, hand painted designer originals, and you name it.

The loveliest gown at the affair was the one worn by the new V.P.'s wife. Mrs. Thornton was a very dignified, but stunning brunette. She had chosen a white silk crepe gown beaded with white crystals and seed pearls. Cut on the bias, the dress clung to her trim figure, then fell gracefully into the folds of a tulip skirt at the hem line. The bodice had raglan sleeves that tapered to nothing at the wrists. The neck was high in the front, the bodice being eased into a mandarin collar. The back was very plain, and was slit to the waist, revealing glimpses of Mrs. Thornton's beautiful back. With her raven black hair the dress was an absolute triumph.

Harry was looking the picture of the young executive, black tie and all. He spotted Tina Murphy across the room and he made his way carefully to her side. Knowing Harry, Tina seemed a little uneasy as he came to her side. "Hello Tina", he ventured, "May I get you some punch?"

Tina felt ashamed of herself when she sensed Harry's effort to be nice. She answered, "Oh, that would be great, Harry." Harry smiled and carefully squeezed through the crowd to the refreshment table. There he poured two cups of punch, a mixture of fruit juices and red wine. Definitely delicious, and definitely dangerous. Harry took the cups carefully and moved back through the crowded room. As he passed the new V.P. and his wife, he was bumped and shoved from behind. Both cups of punch flew into the air and landed at the back of Mrs. Thornton's neck, flooded down her bare back on to the bottom half of her gown where the stain spread out in all directions.

Mrs. Drew, one of the Board of Directors, had been the one to bump Harry, but to cover her 275 pound clumsy move, she shrieked above the gasping of the V.P.'s wife. "My God, Harry, can't you ever watch what you are doing? Look what you have done to Mrs. Thornton's dress."

Harry was devastated. He would never have done anything to hurt anyone. He handed his card to the distraught woman and mumbled, "Please accept my apology and send the cleaning bill to me. I will take care of any repair or permanent damage."

When Harry went back to where Tina was standing, he said, "I'm sorry, Tina, I guess I had better go."

"Wait a minute, Harry" said Tina, "Go? I don't think so. It wasn't your fault. I saw the whole thing. It was Mrs. Drew who was not watching where she was going, she just slammed into you. There was nothing you could do to avoid what happened." Tina frowned as she looked over to the agitated group in the middle of the room. "If you leave now, Harry, I'm going with you. You're not going out of here alone."

"I'm not?" Harry broke into a grin. He had been trying to get a date with Tina Murphy for over a year. She had always been very nice, but distant. She always said "No thank you" to any of Harry's invitations. "You mean you'd leave with me, Tina?" said Harry not believing what was happening.

Tina answered Harry's question with, "Come on, Harry, let's get out of here..."

Harry took Tina home, but before leaving her at her door, they went to a quiet steak house where they sipped a little wine and tried to forget what happened at the reception. There was no big romantic deal, just dinner and pleasant conversation. As they finished their dessert Harry grinned at Tina and said, "You're a nice person Tina Murphy."

"So are you, Harry Wurtz," said Tina with a smile.

When Harry got home he hung up his clothes, put on his sweats and turned on T.V. to see what was on the late news. Suddenly Harry started to sneeze. After several explosive achoo's Harry heard a voice say, "Turn off the T.V., Harry, we need to talk."

Blowing his nose and wiping his eyes, Harry looked in the direction of the voice. Sitting in the big wing back across from Harry was an elf. "Or is it an elf, or, good heavens what is it, he , whatever," stammered Harry to himself.

The elf sat looking at Harry, and he had right beside him what looked like a huge powder puff. "I caused you to sneeze," said the elf looking intently at Harry.

"Why?" said Harry, blowing his nose.

"I had to get your attention, and I was in the process of powdering your rashness. You see, Prilldim is my name, and powdering rashness is my game"

"I don't understand, " said Harry, "I must be imagining."

"No, this is very real, Harry," said Prilldim. "You're finding the reasons you get into so much difficulty."

"You mean you can help me understand why so many negative things happen to me?" said Harry.

"That's right, Harry. You go overboard trying to help when it's not wanted nor needed. Remember Alice? You liked her a lot. But when you told her that she had the hairiest arms you had ever seen on a woman, she didn't care to see you again. She was too embarrassed by your comment," said Prilldim.

"Was that why she got upset at me? Gee, I didn't mean anything by it, "said Harry

"I know that," said Prilldim, "but it was a remark that was too personal and better left unsaid. If I had been there I would have powdered you good!

Remember the time you mentioned to Harriet Truegood that she needed to go on a diet? She had already been on a diet for three weeks and was still so fat that you couldn't tell the difference. Her weight was none of your business, Harry. You never should have mentioned it," said Prilldim, "Another case for the powder."

"Oh my, is that what she's been upset at me for? I just hated to see her getting so heavy, that's all," said Harry. "She's such a nice person and so pretty too."

"Yes, but weight is a touchy subject," said Prilldim. "You can bet your life I would have sent you into a sneezing episode for sure.

Remember the party at Clayton Adam's place?" said Prilldim. "You barged out into the kitchen to help. You weren't asked to participate, nor were you invited into the kitchen. You pushed your way into the swinging doors just as Clayton was pushing his way out. Wham. He had a huge platter of sandwiches, most of which ended up on the floor. Before they could gather them up off the floor, the dog ate a good many. It ended up that there weren't enough sandwiches to go around, and the dog got sick on the Oriental rug in the living room. Harry, you should have stayed out of the kitchen unless you were asked."

"It must be one of the reasons Clayton has never asked me back," said Harry.

"You got it!" said Prilldim.

"You know, I didn't realize how bad the situation had become." said Harry. "I knew there are a lot of people at work who don't care for me. They avoid me and call me 'Hairy Warts' behind my back. Now that I really think about it, I guess I've managed to cause some unpleasantness for just about everyone who works with me. What a disaster. How do I get out of this mess, Prilldim, that is your name isn't it?"

"Yes, that's my name." said Prilldim. "To change your image Harry will take a little effort on your part. There will have to be some basic rules."

Prilldim started to list, "#1, never 'drop in' unexpectedly. People like to plan for company. The very time that you would choose to visit could be the very worst time for the one you would go to see. This would automatically get you off to a bad start.

#2, if you are at a private party, never start to help unless you ask and are given permission, or you are asked to be of assistance.

#3, most of the time it is inappropriate to make personal comments. You will find that most people are uncomfortable with them. Comments about weight or skin blemishes especially. If some one wants your help or opinion, wait until they ask for it.

#4, never never never interrupt. In the first place it is rude, and in the second place you could blow a whole conversation that was very important.

#5, never pry into the affairs of others. If you are asked for advice, that's different, but don't ask questions of a personal nature that are none of your business.

"You see, Harry" said Prilldim, "most of the things to remember are just plain good manners. You know, sort of a 'do unto others' code of ethics."

"I see a lot of things that I have been doing wrong," said Harry, "but I don't see how you are going to help with these problems."

"What I'm going to do is this," said Prilldim. "I'm going to be around you for a while. You won't be able to see me, I don't want to embarrass you, but when you even start to get out of line I will dust you with my powder thoroughly. You'll know I'm around because you will start to sneeze. This will stop you from making a fool of yourself." Prilldim was looking intently into Harry's eyes so as to really bring the point home.

"You mean you will keep me in line? Hey, that sounds great," said Harry. " Will anyone else know?"

"Not unless you tell them," said Prilldim, "and if I were you I'd guard our little secret like the combination to the safe at Fort Knox." Prilldim was smiling now. He liked Harry a lot and was glad to be able to help him.

`"So, when do we start?" asked Harry.

"Right now," said Prilldim." I'm going to disappear, but you will see me a bit later. I may whisper to you now and then, but you won't see me nor will anyone else. Goodbye for now, Harry."

Prilldim sat in the big chair and faded from view.

"Goodbye and thanks," said Harry to the empty chair.

The first time that Harry got powdered was coming into the building at work the next day. He noticed a young lady get in the elevator right ahead of him. The pretty dress that she had on still had the purchase tag hanging out of the sleeve. Harry noticed that the dress had originally been priced at $225, but was marked down to $l05. Quite a savings! Harry started to mention the cleverness of finding such a wonderful bargain, to the young lady, but was suddenly seized with a fit of sneezing.

"Were you saying something to me, Mr. Wurtz?" said the young lady.

"Just that you look exceptionally nice today, Annie," said Harry blowing his nose. "Saved by the sneeze," thought Harry to himself.

"Any comment regarding sale price is inappropriate Harry unless the young lady brings up the subject herself." whispered Prilldim.

Annie turned to Harry and flashed a beautiful smile, "Why, what a nice thing to say. Thank you Mr. Wurtz."

Harry smiled to himself as he gathered up the papers on his desk. He was due in the conference room in a few minutes. He noticed Bill Clark come out of his office with a folder. Before Mr. Clark got to the conference room some papers fell out of his folder unnoticed and landed on the floor right in front of Harry.

Harry hurried to pick up the scattered papers as he walked into the conference room just behind Mr. Clark. He looked down at the papers and started to read. "Personal and Confidential" they were marked. Harry started to read further and was attacked by a horrible sneezing fit. He just walked over to Bill and handed him the papers face down. "You dropped these, Bill," he whispered.

"Oh my gosh, thanks, Harry," said Bill as his face turned red. No one else noticed that Bill had dropped the papers. Bill was grateful for that.

Harry had almost broken rule #5, "don't ever pry into the affairs of others."

All in all, Harry did quite well. He noticed that Mr. Ogden had oatmeal on his tie again, and said nothing.

When the meeting was over Harry made his way back to his own desk. There on his desk was an envelope addressed to him.

Harry opened the letter and read:

Dear Mr. Wurtz;

I am so sorry you left the reception last Friday evening. You see, someone brought to my attention that the accident with the punch was not your fault. You just happened to be in the wrong place at the wrong time

just as I was. You were very sweet to offer to make amends, but it isn't necessary as it has been taken care of.

I hope to see you again under happier circumstances.

Again thank you,

Agnes Thornton.

"What a nice thing for her to do." thought Harry. "She must have sensed that I felt terrible that her dress had been soiled. What a lady!" Harry smiled. "Yes, what a nice thing for her to do."

Harry learned fast and Prilldim really kept at him. Every time he started to embarrass himself, or someone else, Prilldim would let fly with the powder puff and Harry would sneeze instead of getting into trouble.

After a couple of weeks passed, people were noticing the change in Harry. He was becoming quite the gentleman. They did feel sorry, though, that he had developed such a bad allergy. Everyone liked the new Harry, and you know what? So did Harry. He was becoming a very charming individual.

By the time a few months passed Harry had learned his lessons well. Tina Murphy regularly consented to be his date, and life was treating Harry quite well, and vice versa.

One evening as Harry read the newspaper he looked up and over in the big wingback chair he saw Prilldim sitting there smiling at him.

"What?" said Harry. "What have I done wrong this time?"

"You've done nothing wrong, Harry. You've graduated, that's what," said Prilldim. "You don't need me anymore. You have become a charming, gracious, polite, and quite sought after personality about town. Just promise that if you need me you'll let me know."

"How?" asked Harry.

"Just whisper my name." said Prilldim as he faded from view.

Harry sat there in his chair quietly for a few minutes. Then he took off his glasses and wiped his eyes. "I'll miss that little guy," he thought to himself. "This has been a wonderful year. I've always been able to make money, but this year has been the best of all. This year I have learned to make friends." Harry smiled to himself, "Things can only get better."

THE NORNOODLER

Nornoodler works hard at nothing at all
Except to make sure that you're having a ball

He lives in a closet where pleasure is stored,
And there isn't a bit that you can't afford,

He has big laughs and small laughs and joy in a jar,
The joy he spreads on when you're not up to par.

He'll come to a party or come to a dance,
Or any occasion you wish to enhance.

He makes a dull time a sparkling affair,
And sees to enjoyment for everyone there.

Take him along on a job to be done,
With him at your side, it has to be fun!

CHRISTI AND NORNOODLER

The idea of being a cruise director on a major cruise line was the absolute dream of Christi Foster. This job was definitely what she wanted to do. Christi had taken the appropriate courses in college to be able to effectively interact with people of all ages. "No one will go home without a happy experience if I can help it," said Christi to herself as she parked her car in the special dockside lot provided for cruise personnel.

Christi locked all doors after removing her luggage to place it on a folding rack with wheels. After securing to the rack the things she was bringing on the trip, she smiled to herself, tossed the car keys up into the air, and caught them with one hand. Then she placed her keys in her handbag and made her way toward the beautiful big white ship tied up at dock #3. "Well, this is it," Christi whispered to no one in particular. Then she took a deep breath, let it out slowly, and walked up the gangplank.

It was early, and there was a decided nip in the air. Crew members had been notified to be early so that they could stow their own things and make ready for the guests that would soon start boarding. Christi pulled her sweater around her and followed the directions to the small cubicle she would be calling home for the next eight days. She carefully unpacked and settled in all her things. The small quarters demanded organization and Christi was glad she had been warned of the cramped accommodations.

After making room for everything, Christi donned the uniform that she found hanging in her small locker. She checked her mirror. It reflected a very pretty young 23-year old, 5'5", and about 120 pounds with big and very blue eyes and light brown, naturally curly hair. "With the damp sea air I sure am grateful for curly hair," thought Christi to herself. She looked at the mirror smiled and said out loud, "Elizabeth Taylor you're not, but you'll do." Christi locked the door to her small cabin and started up the stairs to the deck where passengers would be coming aboard. The head purser, a gentleman named Allen Bruce, tanned, very tall, thin, and terribly British greeted Christi. "Good morning," he said smiling, "Miss Foster, isn't it?" Christi nodded, and he went on, "You will find what you need in this folder." He handed Christi a blue folder with the cruise line's insignia embossed on the front. "Everything is outlined for you, and what you haven't learned in orientation should be in here. I'm assigning assistant purser, Alexander Olsen, to work with you."

A young man who had been standing nearby stepped forward and extending his hand to Christi said, "Just call me Alex".

"You'll get on just fine," said Mr. Bruce. "Between your own common sense and Alexander here, everything should go smoothly. I have some other people to attend to now. Let me know, Christi, Alex, if you face a problem you can't handle between the two of you." With that Mr. Bruce turned and walked away and left the two of them standing there.

Alex was a blessing. He went through Christi's folder, gave her some pointers, and made some invaluable notes. Basically Christi's job was to be of help at all times, see to it that everyone was having a good time while being a happy example for them. That was just what she intended to do.

There was a lot of excitement as people began arriving. Christi checked them off her list as they boarded and directed them toward their quarters. Then she showed them where to find Alex who was assigning the seating in the dining room. For the most part everything was going great. People were in a good mood as they were looking forward to their leisure time and happy experience on the lovely ocean liner. Then that afternoon things started to fall apart.

Christi was about to welcome aboard a cross looking gentleman in his late fifties. As she held out her hand to welcome him he became agitated. "What do you want, girl?" he shouted when Christi asked his name.

"I want to welcome you aboard, Mr. Finch, and help you find your room, sir." she said.

"What I want from you young lady is to be left alone. I've taken this miserable cruise three times before. I have the same room on the same deck and the same seating in the dining room just as before. Now if you'll step back and get out of my face I'd appreciate it," said Mr. Finch.

Christi's face turned red. She was angry, and hurt, and embarrassed for him. "Yes sir, go right ahead." Mr. Finch swept by her and disappeared into the crowd. "What makes him like that I wonder?" she thought to herself.

As the afternoon went on it seemed there was one unpleasant situation after another. "What's the matter with people anyway," thought Christi to herself, "they're supposed to be going on this cruise to have a good time, to build memories. I sure hope the whole cruise is not going to be like this." Then she looked up into the face of a very angry woman who was pushing her way through the crowd.

"I'm late", the woman yelled, "and it's all your fault!" She came right up to Christi's face and said, "I have never seen such a lack of common sense in anybody like the crew of this ship!"

Christi was shocked. She really didn't know how to contend with this kind of rude behavior. She managed to sputter out, "Your name please?"

"My name is Agnes Feller and the information the bunch of nincompoops at your cruise ship office gave me was incorrect. My papers say I should be here at 4:30. If I had not started out ahead of time to allow for crazy traffic, I would have arrived at 4:30 and the ship would have been on its way out of the harbor. I suppose there's not a single decent place left in the dining room." The fat Mrs. Feller was huffing and puffing her way past Christi.

"Welcome aboard, Mrs. Feller," said Christi, managing a weak smile as she tried to keep her cool. "Your seating assignment will be handled by Mr. Olsen, right over there."

Next coming up the gangplank was a couple who looked edgy as they hauled themselves onto the deck. "Welcome aboard," offered Christi to the unhappy pair that approached her.

"Yeah, sure," said the man. The woman mumbled something under her breath.

"Lets see now", said Christi, looking through her list, "Your name please?"

"Bill and Daisy Clark," said the man looking around with displeasure at everything in sight. "When did they do the last safety inspection on this tub?"

"That information is in a pamphlet in your cabin, sir, or you can arrange to see the engineer once we get under way," said Christi.

Mrs. Clark looked miserable. "Lighten up, Bill," she said. "They wouldn't let an unsafe ship go out with all these people."

"Are you kidding?" Mr. Clark responded. "People would do anything for money, Daisy, you know that. Well we're here, come on we have to find our quarters." Mr. Clark jerked the pamphlet from Christi's hand, took Mrs. Clark by the elbow and moved away grumbling to his wife and to himself.

"That's the last of them, thank goodness," thought Christi to herself. "How can there be so many hateful, unhappy, angry and rude people all in one place? I sure do hope that it won't be impossible to see to it that they all have a good time. I sure have my job cut out for me."

Christi had quite a few encounters that turned out to be very unpleasant. She felt her confidence and self esteem sinking. "What am I doing wrong?" she asked herself. She sat down and put her hands in her lap and just sat glumly thinking about it all.

"What's the matter, Christi? You look like you've lost your best friend." It was Alex, he looked down at Christi, a smile lighting his face.

"Oh Alex, what a welcome sight you are!" exclaimed Christi. "This whole afternoon has been a terrible disaster."

"They were a surly bunch, weren't they," laughed Alex. "It'll be a real challenge, Christi, but it's our job. We'll be up to it when the time calls for it. We have to see to it that we're the good time Charlies on this ship."

"Oh brother," said Christi, "I hope I can measure up."

"You will when the time comes, Christi, you will." With that Alex went down toward his cabin and out of sight.

There were some pleasant people aboard, and that did take some of the sting out of facing the others. Christi made a real effort to treat everyone the same no matter what their attitude, or how they responded.

After a couple of days Christi was really concerned about the reaction to the programs the cruise presented. The cruise line offered wonderful things to do. The ship agenda was a real attempt to entertain, to encourage fitness, to offer the best cuisine, "What more could we do to help them have a good time?" she said to herself as she watched a group laughing over a game of shuffleboard.

Christi headed toward her cabin. "It's me," she thought as she walked down the passageways toward her room. "I'm doing something wrong. But what?" Christi opened the door to her cabin, sat down on the bunk, and then put her head down into the pillow at the head of the bed. She felt her spirit sink into depression, and she was almost in tears as she said to herself, "Why can't I make them all happy? I've tried every trick I know."

"You can't make them all happy," said a voice.

Christi started. She sat up and looked around her cabin. "Who said that?" she demanded. Then she heard a giggle over by her desk.

"I said it. Me, Nornoodler. My specialty is happiness, and even though we can work a little magic, you can't win 'em all. You see, Christi, the trouble with most people is that wherever they go, there they are!" said the funny looking little creature. "You can't change that. It takes a little magic."

"I don't understand, " said Christi. "And where did you get a name like Nornoodler, and where did you come from anyway, or am I hallucinating?"

"Whoa," said Nornoodler. "One question at a time. First of all, most people take their unhappy attitude with them. If they were miserable at home, most times they are miserable wherever they go. Secondly, my name is Nornoodler, and I come from the Island of Corkle. Nornoodlers specialize in happiness. Now, you see, what goes on in another person's head is something that only that person has control of. They are the only ones who can really change their own thinking. If they have decided to be unhappy, there really isn't much you can do to change it, but don't let it influence the way you think or feel."

"Are you trying to tell me that some people are unhappy on purpose?" asked Christi "How can they be unhappy deliberately?"

"Easy," said Nornoodler." All they have to do is feed their minds on a steady diet of unforgiveness, resentment, jealously, hate, and dishonesty just to name a few attitudes for unhealthy thinking. Once these thoughts are embedded in their minds, it's darn near impossible for them to smile."

"What you mean is that they have programmed themselves for unhappiness?" asked Christi.

"Exactly, Christi," said Nornoodler, "but I can help if you give me the O.K."

"Just how are you going to do that?" questioned Christi.

"Well, you see," said Nornoodler, "I live in a closet where pleasure is stored. I have big laughs and small laughs and joy in a jar. The joy I spread on when you're not up to par."

Christi looked at Nornoodler long and hard. "I'm imagining this. The job is getting to me," she thought to herself. Then she said, "But how? I mean what exactly do you do?"

Nornoodler brought out a big pink paint brush. "We're going to spread joy up to the maximum, and paint the whole ship with fun. We're going to brush happiness all over the place. You'll see. Come on, Christi, follow me." As Nornoodler moved out of Christi's cabin he slowly disappeared and Christi was all alone, but wait—Nornoodler was not gone, he was just invisible!

Christi moved down the halls where there were staterooms on both sides. She could hear Mrs. Feller down the hall screaming at a steward. "What do you think I'm paying for? When I say pink sheets I don't mean blue!" Her face was red and she was waving her be-jeweled hands frantically. All of a sudden she looked up and saw Christi. Christi heard a "swoosh" and the expression on Mrs. Feller's face changed 100%. "Oh well," Mrs. Feller said to the steward, flashing him her most dazzling smile, "it really doesn't matter, young man. Don't bother changing the sheets. Thanks for your trouble, and here's a little something for you," she said, handing him a twenty dollar bill. The steward gaped at her in disbelief, gave her a quick "yes maam!" and hurried on down the hall.

Christi stopped at Mrs. Feller's door. "We're going to have a get acquainted get-together up on B deck. It's going to be fun. Why not join us?" Christi smiled at the woman.

"Oh, my dear, I'd love to. All of a sudden I feel like a little fun and excitement. Some getting acquainted activity would do me good." Mrs. Feller was fussing around her cabin. "I'll see you up there, Christi," she said happily.

"Only the Nornoodler could have done that," said Christi to herself.

As Christi moved around the ship she was aware of the attitude of others changing. Some of the ones who had been surly and hateful were suddenly jovial and outgoing. "Nornoodler is walking right ahead of me, spreading joy as we go," Christi giggled. " This is great," she whispered to herself.

When Christi arrived up on B deck she went outside to get some air. She noticed Mr. Finch wrapped up like a cigar store Indian, sitting in a deck lounge chair She didn't say anything to him at first because she didn't want to bother him. Then again Christi heard the familiar "swoosh". She saw Mr. Finch sit up and open his eyes. He looked over at Christi and broke into a big smile, "Well hello, young lady, are you enjoying the cruise so far?"

Christi was surprised to hear Mr. Finch say hello, and then she realized that the Nornoodler had most likely smeared him on his way by.

"Yes, I am," she said, then with a smile she added, "We're having a get together in the B deck lounge, why not join us?"

"You know, why not?" said Mr. Finch, "I've been sitting around sulking long enough. Count on me, Miss Foster, I'll be there!"

"Thanks, Nornoodler," said Christi in a whisper.

"You're welcome," answered the Nornoodler in her ear.

As Christi entered the B deck lounge she could see that the Nornoodler had been there first. The whole place was jumping. As she entered the room Nornoodler was certainly spreading joy up to the maximum. "Wow, what a party," thought Christi to herself.

"How'd you do this?" It was Alex. He stood there taking in all the festivities. "Christi, every hard nose on the ship is here. They're laughing and having a great old time. What did you do?" he asked.

"Do?" asked Christi coyly, "I didn't do anything. I just said be happy and I guess they are. Great party isn't it?"

Alex went on. "Look at the Clarks over there with Hank Gunther our engineer. I overheard Hank ask Mr. Clark if he'd like a tour of the engine room, he seldom does that. There's something in the air, Christi."

"I agree," said Christi. "I'd call it a sort of magic."

"Yeah," said Alex. "It's a sort of magic all right. Hope it keeps it up for the whole cruise."

Christi looked around the room. Mrs. Feller was doing some serious fancy dancing with a gentleman her age, they were having a glorious time. The Clarks were on their feet and dancing too. Then Christi couldn't believe her eyes. Mr. Finch had some younger lady in his arms and was dancing up a storm. Everyone was having a fabulous time. "Nornoodler has done wonders for this group," thought Christi. "Now, how do I keep things rolling?" she wondered to herself.

Alex came back to her side. "No kidding, Christi, what happened? The whole group here has changed. Seriously, how did you do it?" he asked.

"Alex, you should know that the only one who can make an individual happy is themselves. I could only offer a list of fun things to do. Whether the offer was taken or not, was up to each person. No one really has the power to make someone else happy, that's something one has to do for their self, and It starts with loving yourself"

"Well said," whispered the Nornoodler in Christi's ear. "Meet me outside, I need to say good-bye."

"Where are you going?" said Christi when they got outside.

"I have to spread the joy around, Christi," said the Nornoodler. "Things seem to be going forward pretty well. Look at that crowd in there. They're having a blast!"

"Wonderful!" said Christi. "So how do I keep them happy without you?"

"Don't you see, Christi," said Nornoodler, "You don't keep them happy. The little magic I used will help them all find the happiness within themselves. That has to happen before they can have a good time. It'll work, you'll see." Nornoodler gave Christi his funny lopsided smile. "Be happy yourself, Christi, it's catching. Bye for now, I'll check back next cruise." With that, Nornoodler was gone.

"What are you doing out here talking to yourself?" It was Alex.

"Just enjoying the beauty, Alex," answered Christi.

"Come on back in, Christi, and join the fun," said Alex.

There were eight more days. Nornoodler had set the mood,

everyone was in a "get acquainted" frame of mind. The fun was catching, the laughter was infectious, and Christi was having the time of her life watching others enjoy themselves.

Then it was time to say good bye to all the new friends she had made. Christi stood and smiled as each person said good-bye and walked down the gangplank.

"Well done, Miss Foster," said a voice at Christi's elbow. It was Mr. Bruce . "I don't recall any Cruise Director doing as well as you have your first time out. Everyone is thrilled with the trip, even Mr. Finch. Are you going to share your secret?" Mr. Bruce smiled.

"To quote a friend, Mr. Bruce, it's just a matter of being happy yourself. It's catching, you know," said Christi.

REFLECTIONS

There are many more Porple, too many to mention,
If we left yours out, it was not our intention.

You might find it fun to make up your own,
A "tailor made" Porple to call your own clone.

Then you might look him over and see in your mirror,
Your way to improvement made a bit clearer.

You can be your own critic, then say "Hold the phone,"
"That wasn't my doing, that guy was my clone."

But remember! The fellow you live with is you.
Your Judge and your Jury, whatever you do.

We are all someone special, and we're put here to learn,
That whatever we are is something we earn!

AUNT LUCINDA'S LEGACY

Heather Lockwood sat in the light of the breakfast nook windows watching the birds in the garden as her mind went over the events of the past two years.

The position at City College was perfect. When Heather came to Santa Barbara two years before, she was not sure that she would want to stay. Everything seemed to work out right from the beginning. Teaching Home Economics was what she had always wanted to do, and Heather felt she was preparing for the time when she would have a home of her own.

Aunt Lucinda had insisted that Heather move in and live with her. The big old mansion on upper Garden Street, although in need of refurbishing, was charming, and Aunt Lucinda said "there's room to spare, please stay." Heather was the grandchild of her only brother, and if she was to be in Santa Barbara there would always be room for her.

Heather had not seen her Great Aunt Lucinda since she was nine years old, but when she arrived on Lucinda's McDowell's doorstep there were greetings and hugs just as though there had been no time in between.

Every time Heather mentioned she should get a place of her own, Aunt Lucinda protested. "Why, Heather? I have so much room, and besides you have brought a breath of fresh air into this big old musty house."

So Heather stayed. Aunt Lucinda had a couple who "lived in" to help keep things up. Mr. and Mrs. Lassiter had been at the Garden Street address for 17 years. They were both delightful, and considered themselves very lucky to find a place to live plus employment in such a happy environment.

Almost two years went by and Heather and Aunt Lucinda became very close. Heather insisted upon paying room and board and Aunt Lucinda accepted finally. She was proud and happy that Heather wanted to pay her own way.

During the time that she taught at Santa Barbara City College, Heather met David Clay at a faculty get acquainted gathering. David was an instructor in the drafting department. Heather had seen David on the City College campus and had wondered who the tall, tan blonde was. He was very attractive, and somehow the big brown eyes were always full of mischief.

David and Heather were both from the Mid-west and they hit it off right away. There was an unspoken devotion to one another, and they knew that their relationship was going to be permanent. David also enjoyed Aunt Lucinda, and became a regular at the mansion on Garden Street.

The tears welled up in Heather's big blue eyes as she looked back at the moment three weeks ago when the doctor told her Aunt Lucinda had passed away. "It was sudden, and easy, and it was time, after all Lucinda McDowell was 94 years old."

Heather brushed the raven black hair away from her face and gazed out the breakfast nook window, wondering, "What now?" Aunt Lucinda's attorney had called right after the funeral and told her to come to his office this afternoon at one o'clock. "He probably wants to know how soon I can move," she thought to herself. "Or is there something else he wants me for? Why? What's the hurry? I need this time to look for a place to live."

One o'clock however, found Heather at the attorney's office waiting to be called.

"Miss Lockwood, Mr. Adams will see you now." The receptionist interrupted Heather's thoughts. She held out her hand to indicate "This way please." Heather followed and found herself in a comfortable office that seemed to be all wood, leather, and bookcases. Behind the big polished desk sat a very pleasant looking middle-aged man.

"Miss Lockwood, thank you for coming" he said, "Please have a chair. I'll get right to the point. Your Aunt Lucinda has been my client for many years. May I express my sympathy, she was a great lady"

"Yes, she was," murmured Heather wondering what he was getting at.

He went on. "She has left a will leaving everything, the house on Garden Street and the assets listed here in this folder to you, Heather Lockwood."

Heather's mouth fell open. "She left it to me? But, are you sure? Just me alone?"

Mr. Adams smiled. "It's all here exactly the way she wanted it. I will need you to sign a few papers, just a formality. Some of these financial reports are a little complicated. If you have any questions I'll be happy to help explain things, so that you will have a full understanding of the whole estate finances. Just call anytime and we can set up an appointment."

"Thanks, I'll most likely need you, Mr. Adams," said Heather "Has there been any provision made for the Lassiters? They've been so loyal to Aunt Lucinda. Surely there's—"

"Nothing as far as I know. I feel certain that your Great Aunt Lucinda will want you to decide what to do regarding the Lassiters," said Mr. Adams.

"Oh dear." Heather was suddenly concerned. "This is a lot of responsibility." The house, the Lassiters, the listed assets that would have to be explained to her. Heather's mind whirled with questions.

Mr. Adams went on. "I would hate to see you sell that lovely house in today's real estate market. Prices are down. That house has some unique features, and it is a 'one of a kind' residence in this area. Your Great Uncle Ely brought some of the wood for the paneling halfway around the world. The pink marble in the upstairs bathrooms is very special. Some of the chandeliers and sconces around the house are irreplaceable. And then there's the front hall mirror. That's a story in itself. Do take time, Miss Lockwood, to think about these things before you consider placing the house on the market." Mr. Adams placed his fingertips together as if in prayer and looked at Heather over his glasses. "Take these papers home and take time to go over them at your leisure." He handed the folder to Heather, who was sure her knocking knees could be heard in the outer office.

"Thank you, Mr. Adams. May I make an appointment at this time for next Tuesday? That will give me the weekend to go over things."

When she got home, Heather parked in the driveway, and walked around to the front walk. As she approached the big old mansion with slow and deliberate steps, Heather was spellbound by its regal beauty. It was as if she had never seen it before. The patterned brickwork at her feet captured her gaze, and she noticed the intricate design of the bricks, and how the pattern repeated all the way up to the steps of the house. Heather studied the lovely rose trees on each side of the walkway, stopping to savor the fragrance of one or two blossoms, then progressed slowly up to the front entrance. The exquisite etching on the oval windows of the heavy oak doors held her attention for the very first time. She took out her key, opened the door, and found herself in the front foyer staring at her own reflection in the large Victorian mirror in front of her.

Heather stood there for a few moments, transfixed by her own image in the beautiful old looking glass.

"Well, Heather, what's to become of us all now that you are in charge?" The mirror was actually speaking to Heather. She was shocked and her practical mind was bent a little.

"I don't know yet. I haven't gone over all the papers that Mr. Adams gave me." She answered before she thought. "This old house is a huge responsibility. It's going to take a lot of money and effort to put it into shape, and after I get it refurbished, then what do I do?" Heather was confused, talk to a mirror? Was the day too long, was the sun too warm? "Am I getting a little bit nuts?" Heather wondered all these things as she continued to look at the mirror.

"Take a look at yourself," said the mirror.

Heather stared into the mirror and saw a change. She saw a Heather very comfortable with herself and with her surroundings. She became curious and asked the mirror. "What do I do with all of this? Am I losing my mind?"

"Heather," the mirror began, "you have a lovely home with furnishings that would be the envy of any antique dealer. Why not turn this fabulous old house into a Bed and Breakfast? Your expertise in Home Economics will be invaluable."

Heather looked at the mirror in amazement. "If I had the money it would be an incredible idea. I still need to go over some information to see if your idea is feasible. Other than that, Mirror, I love the idea—I love it."

Mrs. Lassiter suddenly appeared in the hallway. "What is it Miss Heather? I heard you talking to someone. Will there be company for supper?"

"I don't know yet, Mrs. Lassiter" said Heather. "I was just sorta talking to myself." But Heather did take a long quizzical look at the big Victorian mirror.

Heather went upstairs to her room and called David. "Can you come over, David? It's rather important. This has been quite a day."

"What's up, Heather? Where have you—"

Heather interrupted David. "I don't want to talk about it on the phone. Just come on over as soon as you can. Supper is ready and there's plenty. It's ready now and waiting. Oh hurry, David."

"Sounds exciting, I'll be right there," said David.

It was just 15 minutes later that Heather heard the sound of David's diesel truck pulling into the driveway. She hurried down the stairs to meet him. "You'll never believe what happened to me today, David," she said breathlessly.

"It must be pretty wild," smiled David. "What is it Heather? What's going on?"

"Remember I got the call from Mr. Adams, Aunt Lucinda's attorney? Well, he informed me that I'm the sole heir to everything. The house here, a variety of investments, everything. Oh David, what am I going to do with this museum? I don't know anything about houses and construction and all that." Heather told David about her idea for a bed and breakfast.

"Well, I do. I have been in construction all my life," said David. "Don't worry, Heather, I'll help. Come on in the house, we'll talk about it." They moved up the walk and into the foyer. David suddenly stopped and stared at the big Victorian mirror. "Heather, I never really looked at that mirror before this. It's beautiful," he said.

"David that mirror is weird," said Heather avoiding any glance in the direction of the mirror. She pulled at David's arm. "Come on for heaven's sake, I'm hungry."

As they moved into the dining room Heather told the Lassiters what had happened at the attorneys. She could tell that they were relieved to know that she wanted them to stay.

"I don't know how it's all going to work out, but we'll do it together somehow," Heather smiled at them all. "Let's eat supper now, we'll think about it later."

The dining room was a wonderful combination of very special collectables. The upper doors of the mahogany sideboard were a beautiful stained glass in a tulip pattern. They had been designed to match the imported chandelier over the inlaid mahogany table in the center of the room.

Supper was always served in the dining room. Unless the weather was unbearably hot, Aunt Lucinda always lit the fireplace. The flickering light from the fireplace, plus the candles, bathed the room with a romantic glow. Heather, too, had become accustomed to properly served evening meals in this lovely room. She thought to herself, "We'll keep things as Aunt Lucinda would have them as long as we can."

The chairs were all matching hand carved pieces from Uncle Ely's travel adventures. They were truly lovely and the floral needlepoint on the seats and backs added a regal touch.

Above the fireplace hung a portrait of Aunt Lucinda at about age 40. How stunning she was. Heather's eyes misted looking up at the beautiful woman who was so very special. As David and Heather dined, they said very little. It was enough to be where they were enjoying a delicious meal in beautiful surroundings.

All of a sudden David said, "Look, Heather, the little Cupid on the right side of the fireplace is crooked."

"So it is," answered Heather. She got up from her chair and moved closer to the fireplace mantle. The Cupid was part of a design that appeared to be holding up the mantle. "Come here, David, and look at this. The little Cupid turns." Heather turned the little artifact, and she heard a scraping sound. "Good heavens, David, this whole panel is moving."

The two stood in amazement as the right-hand panel slid back revealing a compartment with several shelves and a safe. There were boxes full of helpful household records, which Heather was thrilled to see. They listed who to call for what, etc. All of Aunt Lucinda's records for the care and upkeep of the property were there and up to date.

"Oh, David, look—everything we need to start rebuilding," said Heather.

"We?" asked David.

"We!" said Heather. "David, I couldn't possibly do all this alone."

"Why Heather Lockwood," grinned David," is this a proposal?"

Heather blushed to the roots of her hair. "Call it whatever you want, David, I need you."

David and Heather talked 'till almost one o'clock. When they said good night David stood in the front hall and looked back at the mirror.

He could have sworn that the mirror said "Good night, David."

"I must be very tired or that mirror is weird," he said to himself as he went down the front walk toward his truck.

Heather stayed in the dining room for a while going over records and information about the house. The combination to the safe was in one of the ledgers. "I'll wait until tomorrow," thought Heather "I've had enough excitement for one day."

The next morning as Heather came down the front stairs, she heard Mrs. Lassiter in a conversation in the front hall. Mrs. Lassiter was talking to the mirror. "She knows about the mirror too," said Heather to herself. She stood quietly and listened. Mrs. Lassiter was talking.

"But Miss Heather has so much on her mind right now," she was saying. "I can't bother her with my ambitions at this time."

"Now is as good a time as any," said the mirror. "Heather is seeing her dreams come true, you have every right to see your own success. Ask her, I think you'll be surprised."

Heather cleared her throat as she came down the last two steps. "Well, good morning Mrs. Lassiter." she said.

"Morning, Miss Heather. The coffee is ready."

"Good, let's have it together in the breakfast nook," said Heather.

Heather sat down and Mrs. Lassiter poured coffee for both of them. "You know," said Heather, "I went over a lot of the finances early this morning, and I think that it just may be financially possible to turn this lovely old home into a Bed and Breakfast. What do you think? It will mean extra work for you and we may have to hire more help."

"I think it's a lovely idea," said Mrs. Lassiter clasping her hands together.

"We'll all have our own specialty. Do you have a talent that you'd like to share Mrs. Lassiter?" asked Heather.

"My pies!" You know Miss Heather I'd like to offer my pies for sale," said Mrs. Lassiter.

"Wonderful," smiled Heather. "Your pies are certainly exceptional, and we'll feature them in the dining room at breakfast. You'll be developing your own little business on the side."

"I was talking it over with, ah- er -a friend," Mrs. Lassiter didn't want to admit that she was getting advice from a mirror. "This friend feels that this could be my way to improve myself."

"I couldn't agree more." said Heather.

Heather and David both took leaves of absence from their teaching jobs, and the remodeling of the great house on Garden Street got under way. It was November and Heather wanted to be able to advertise and open their doors starting in May of the next year.

In February David and Heather were married. Just a small wedding at the house with their minister in charge and their friends around them. It was a good decision, financially and otherwise. David's building expertise was invaluable. No nook was spared. Everything in the house was checked over and brought up to snuff. They used the lovely old hand embroidered linens, and they found charming antique knickknacks everywhere. They put as many old pieces to good use as they could. There were vases, small family pictures to bring a nostalgic smile, and dresser sets, complete with shoe button hooks to make things look like home, the way it was at the turn of the century.

Mr. Lassiter had gone to work in the garden, the place he loved best. He asked Heather if he could put fresh flowers every day in as many rooms as possible. He didn't want anyone "messing" with "his" garden. He was the only one who knew where all the bulbs were buried. Heather was delighted.

She had been putting it off. It was March, and Heather still hadn't investigated all the holdings in the safe in the dining room. "Today is the day, "she announced to herself one morning. She pulled up the little Cupid and found herself staring into the shelves of the cupboard. As she went through the box of papers she found an envelope with her name on it. There was almost twenty thousand dollars in cash. There was a note too, and a key. The note read:

"Dear Heather:

I couldn't bring myself to accept money from you for staying here. Your love has filled this house with so many precious moments. This old lady couldn't feel closer to you if you were her own granddaughter. This money will come in handy in doing the projects I know you will want to do when I'm gone.

The enclosed key is to the cedar box in the back of the closet in the master bedroom. Pull back the winter things and you'll find a small compartment. The box is there.

Thank you my dear for the sunshine you brought to us all. Take care of this lovely old house which is now yours. Fill it with love and children, and be blessed with many happy years within these walls.

I love you.

Lucinda McDowell."

Heather brushed the tears away as she hurried upstairs. Her curiosity was overwhelming. She took the cedar box from the shelf and could hardly carry it to the writing table by the window. "What's in this?" she wondered to herself. She inserted the key and shut her eyes as she pulled up the lid.

The box was filled with little paper rolls neatly stacked. In Aunt Lucinda's handwriting she read.

"Here Heather is your ace in the hole or your umbrella for a rainy day. It is for you and David to do with as you will when you get married. Your Uncle Ely, as he traveled the world collected gold coins from everywhere. The whole collection is here. I hope it will bring you happiness. Spend it my dear, gathered dust is worth nothing. Love, Aunt L."

Heather sat at the table and the tears rolled down her cheeks. "Oh, how I do miss her," she said to herself.

By summer the house was ready for guests. The old mansion gleamed with new paint and clean windows with bright starched lace curtains. The gardens were manicured, and there were flowers blooming everywhere. Parking space accommodations were in the back. They had to move one of the big pepper trees, but there was a parking space for every room.

The sign in front read: "Lucinda's Legacy, a Bed and Breakfast. A Place Where Love Is." then in smaller letters "Featuring Mrs. Lassiter's Pies."

David and Heather found that the Victorian mirror in the front hall spoke to many. Always it gave encouragement for pursuing the dream that each guest carried in their heart, and the encouragement to believe in themselves. Many mentioned the mirror, but none really explained why it was special. Many of the guests became "regulars" and they always spent a little more time in the front hall than was necessary before coming into the parlor to register.

The bed and breakfast on upper Garden Street became the place to visit on a trip through Santa Barbara. Rooms were booked weeks in advance, and nearly every guest ordered one of Mrs. Lassiter's pies to go.

In closing it is safe to say, they lived happily ever after.

.

TAYLOR AWAKENS

Taylor awoke suddenly. He was back in the newsroom. The silence was deafening, and the clock on the wall said 9:30 a.m. He shook his head "I must have fallen asleep." He thought. "What a wild dream! Surely it was a dream of some sort. It was wonderful, certainly worth reporting if it was real. Even if it wasn't real, it's worth sharing."

Taylor slowly gathered his things together and prepared to leave. His eyes fell on the papers stacked for the morning's broadcast. The Corkle story was on top and laying on the stack of papers was a blue feather.

"Wow..." he whispered.

EPILOGUE

The Porple from Corkle don't exist for escape
They're just you in a form, they're just your own traits.

They stop us from thinking we're victims of fate,
And just make us stop and evaluate.

So take them and use them, for this they all wait.
We'll be better people, it isn't too late!

Lightning Source UK Ltd.
Milton Keynes UK
UKHW051058191020
371533UK00024B/249